Hi, Diary,

I can't believe that Landon actually wanted to hang with ME at the mall. ☺ At first, I was kind of worried because he wasn't acting like he wanted to talk to me. Then I realized—duh!—he was probably as nervous as I was. Will I ever stop feeling so scared around him?

But I've got bigger issues to deal with than Landon. I've got only one more week with Ally. Which means that all my best friends have only one more week together to get Bluetopia going. So the two most important things right now are:

1. Friends (Ally, Chloe, and Jasper)

2. Bluetopia

Landon can wait. He has to.

B-Z Zee

BOOK FOUR

Mixed Messages

By

Tina Wells

Illustrations by Michael Segawa

HARPER

An Imprint of HarperCollinsPublishers

Mixed Messages

Library of Congress Cataloging-in-Publication Data
Wells, Tina.
    Mixed messages / Tina Wells ; illustrations by Michael Segawa. —1st ed.
        p.   cm. — (Mackenzie Blue ; 4)
    Summary: Mackenzie and her friends create a new online social
networking site which creates some unforeseen problems, as she is also trying
to figure out if she has a crush on one of her best friends, how to deal with the
jealousy of one of her bandmates, and her fears over her mother's pregnancy.
    ISBN 978-0-06-158319-3 (pbk.)
    [1. Middle schools—Fiction.   2. Musical groups—Fiction.   3. Music—
Fiction.   4. Interpersonal relations—Fiction.   5. Online social networks—
Fiction.   6. Schools—Fiction.]   I. Segawa, Michael, ill.   II. Title.
PZ7.W46846Mi 2010   2010004596
[Fic]—dc22   CIP
                                                                        AC

Typography by Alison Klapthor
13 14 15 16   OPM   10 9 8 7 6 5 4 3 2 1

First paperback edition, 2013

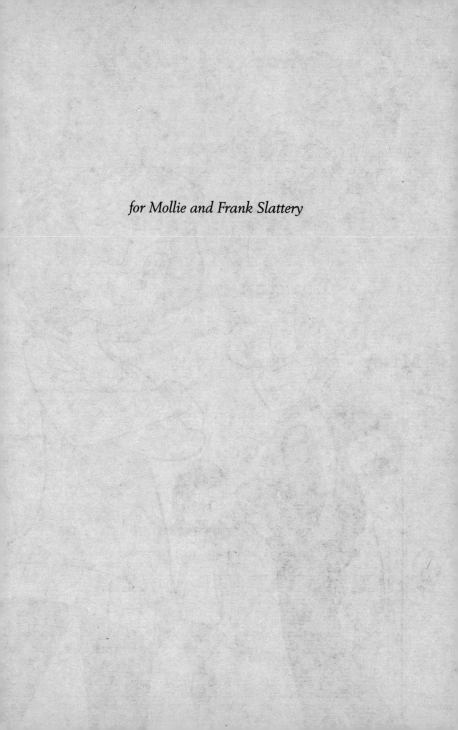

for Mollie and Frank Slattery

BOOK FOUR

Mixed Messages

1

Bluetopia

"I am soooo happy to have electricity and cell phones again," Mackenzie Blue Carmichael said to her friends.

"And warm showers," Zee's BFF, Ally Stern, agreed, sucking a Mocha Chiller through a straw.

"I don't know," Chloe Lawrence-Johnson replied in her southern accent. "I kind of miss being in the wilderness."

"Oh, I didn't mind being in the wilderness," Zee said. "I just don't think all the bugs and dirt needed to be there, too." She brushed off her red kimono tunic as if she were flicking away invisible grime.

"Isn't that kind of the point?" Jasper Chapman asked. "Don't bugs and dirt go with the wilderness?"

The four friends were sitting on the patio of the Brookdale Mall Café, reminiscing about their seventh-grade science field trip to Brookdale Mountain.

"All I'm saying is, I hope the eighth-grade field trip is to a spa," Zee explained.

"No, you don't." Chloe laughed. "Admit it. You had a great time."

Ally leaned closer to Zee and flashed a smile. "After all, I got to be there." Ally was visiting from Paris, where she had moved over the summer. She and Zee had been BFFs since before kindergarten and missed each other tons now that they lived so far apart. When Ally surprised Zee with a visit the week before, Zee was so excited to have all her friends together.

Zee rolled her eyes. "Okay, I had fun. But don't tell my parents. They're threatening to take Adam and me camping in the spring."

"I bet it would be awesome to go camping with your brother," Chloe said.

Zee shrugged. "Well . . . I don't know about that, but Adam's not really the problem. I think I might spontaneously combust if I ever have to go a week without the internet again."

"That would certainly be messy," Jasper said.

"Even without cell phones and the internet, I thought the week went by incredibly fast," Ally said.

"I hope this week doesn't," Zee told her. "You have to go back to Paris on Saturday."

"Don't remind me," Ally said, frowning. "I'm going to miss you so much." She turned to Jasper and Chloe. "You guys, too."

"I can't believe I'm going to have to say good-bye all over again," Zee said. "I'm going to be way sad."

"At least you'll still be able to IM and email," Chloe pointed out. Her green eyes sparkled with encouragement.

"I guess," Zee said with a sigh, "but it's not the same. Paris and California are in totally different time zones. So when I'm just getting to school, Ally's day is almost over."

"And by the time Zee gets home from school, it's time for me to go to sleep," Ally put in.

"When we finally do connect, we have to spend so much time catching up on what our friends did and said," Zee explained.

"And then we are usually interrupted before we get to the juicy stuff."

"It would be so much easier if we could just start with that," Zee added.

"Like you can on Facebook and MySpace?" Chloe said.

"What do you mean?" Zee asked.

"You can post pictures and updates and other information about yourself," Chloe said.

"Right!" Zee agreed. "Adam is constantly posting what he's doing every minute of every day—as if anyone cares."

"We wouldn't have to spend a lot of time filling one another in when we finally do chat," Ally said. "Our posts would keep our friends up-to-date, and they could read them whenever they wanted."

"You know so much about it, Chloe," Zee said. "Do you have a Facebook page?"

Chloe shook her head so fast, her thick ponytail nearly whipped her face. "No way! My parents won't let me join Facebook or MySpace until I'm older."

"I think my parents would," Ally said, looking hopefully at Zee.

"Count me out," Zee told her, and her shoulders slumped. "I already asked. Facebook rules say you have to be fourteen to have an account, and my parents *love* to follow rules."

"Those big sites make my mum nervous," Jasper put in matter-of-factly. "That's why I'm building my own social networking site for my friends back in England." Jasper had moved to Brookdale from London over the summer.

"*Excuse* me," Chloe said, putting down her strawberry-kiwi vitamin water. "You're *making* a site like that?"

"Well . . . yes," Jasper said.

"Cool beans!" Zee cheered. "But how come you never told us you were into computers?"

"I suppose because you never asked," Jasper answered. "And I didn't think it was important."

"It is soooo important," Zee said.

Ally nodded. "Yeah, very."

"Why?" Jasper asked.

"Because we're your best friends, and it's like you're keeping a major secret from us," Zee explained.

Jasper turned to Chloe with pleading eyes. Behind his round wire-rimmed glasses, they looked as though they

were screaming, "Save me!"

"Don't look at me," Chloe protested. "I can't believe we didn't know."

"That's not how it works with my mates in England," Jasper said.

"It's because they're boys," Chloe said. "Girls share everything."

"Yeah, if you're going to hang out with us," Ally began, "you have to, too."

"Fine." Jasper threw his arms in the air, nearly knocking over his half-full glass of milk. "I'm almost finished building the site. It's going to be by invitation only." Zee, Ally, and Chloe stared expectantly at him. "Of course, you three will be invited."

"Awesome!" Chloe cheered. "We finally get to meet your British friends!"

"I love the idea," Zee said. "Can I help you come up with stuff to put on it—stuff girls might like, too?"

"Sure! I was thinking about calling it Bluetopia anyway," Jasper blurted out.

"Bluetopia?" Zee could feel her face redden.

"As in *Mackenzie* Blue?" Ally asked.

Jasper shook his head slightly as if he hadn't realized he'd actually said the name out loud. "Uh . . . yeah," he stammered, looking down. "You know, because you're going to help, and I don't want to take all the credit."

"Jasper definitely doesn't like to be the center of attention the way that Zee does!" Chloe jumped in.

"Hey! What's that supposed to mean?" Zee laughed.

"You know what I mean," Chloe said. "You want to be a rock star. Jasper would rather be . . . a . . . a . . ."

"Yes?" Jasper prompted. "Go on."

"You know . . . a thing that's *not* shiny and bright and gets a lot of attention."

Jasper tugged at the collar of his green polo shirt. "A rock?"

"Uh . . . lemme get back to you on that," Chloe said. Then she turned to Zee and squeaked, "Help!"

Zee sucked the last drop of mocha through her straw. "I've gotta get back home," she said. "My mom says I have to clean my room before our spa appointment at Wink today."

Ally laughed. "Ginny said she's never seen anyone who can turn a spotless room into a demolition zone in less than twenty-four hours," she told Jasper and Chloe.

"I had some help getting it messy," Zee said, looking sideways at her friend.

"I'll help you clean it up," Ally said.

"And I will work on the code for the site," Jasper said.

The group got up from their table and headed to the bike rack. They unlocked their bikes and began to climb on as a gray minivan pulled up to the curb. It had barely stopped when the door slid open.

"You're not leaving, are you?" Conrad Mitori called to Zee and her friends as he stepped onto the sidewalk.

Marcus Montgomery landed next to him. "Hang out with us for a while," he said. Conrad and Marcus were also Brookdale Academy seventh graders.

Zee looked at Chloe. Chloe had a crush on Marcus, and Zee could tell that Chloe would have liked to stay longer. "Sorry, guys. We have to go home. We're getting manicures later," Zee explained.

"You're choosing manicures over us?" Marcus protested. He slapped his hand on his chest and staggered as though he'd just been wounded.

Conrad flapped his hands. "Well, we know how important it is to have perfect nails," he teased. "Not!"

Zee laughed. "Stop it, you g—" She paused when she saw Landon Beck, the boy who she had had a huge crush on since forever, come out of the van, too.

"Hi!" Landon said, staring right at Zee.

"Oh . . . uh . . . hi . . . ," Zee stammered. "What's up?"

Landon shoved his hands in the pockets of his shorts and shrugged. "Not much," he said.

"Umm . . . are you going to hang out at the mall?" Zee asked.

Landon nodded so that his blond bangs bounced against his tan forehead. "Yeah," he said. Zee felt like fireworks were going off in her head, but Landon looked so calm. "You want to hang with us?"

"I can't," Zee said.

"Oh, okay."

Think of something to say, Zee told herself. *Anything.*

Luckily, Ally saved Zee. "You know,

manicures aren't just for girls," she told Marcus and Conrad. "You guys could probably use one after a week in the woods."

"Are you getting one, Jasper?" Marcus asked.

"Oh no," Jasper said quickly. "The girls are on their own."

Conrad put his arm around Jasper. "So stick with us."

"I'm afraid I have to decline," Jasper said. "There's something I have to work on at home." He climbed onto his bike.

"Are you heading off to save a rain forest?" Conrad asked.

"Or planting one?" Marcus joked. Jasper spent a lot of time on environmental issues at Brookdale Academy. Along with Chloe, he had created a garden on campus where they could grow vegetables for the cafeteria, then turn the food scraps into compost for the plant beds.

"No, it has nothing to do with the environment," Jasper explained as he waved good-bye.

Conrad turned to Marcus and shrugged. "I thought everything he did had something to do with the environment."

Ally began to pedal away, too. "Good-bye."

"Later!" Marcus shouted.

Zee looked at Landon. "Bye," she said.

Landon smiled. "See ya!"

Zee's bike started to wobble. She straightened it up and followed her friends, hoping that she could make it out of the boys' sight without doing something klutzy like falling off.

"Well . . . that was interesting," Ally said as they headed away from the mall.

"Very," Chloe agreed.

"What?" Zee asked.

"You know . . . Landon," Ally explained.

Zee stared at her friends sternly, hoping they'd get the message. Zee hadn't ever told Jasper that she had a crush on Landon.

Chloe didn't pick up on the hint. "As if you didn't know," Chloe said.

"Didn't know what?" Jasper asked.

"It's nothing," Zee quickly jumped in. Her red extra-high Converse sneakers pushed faster on the bike's pedals. This didn't feel like the time to spill the news about her crush to Jasper. "It was just interesting to see all the guys there."

Hi, Diary,

I can't believe that Landon actually wanted to hang with ME at the mall. ☺ At first, I was kind of worried because he wasn't acting like he wanted to talk to me. Then I realized—duh!—he was probably as nervous as I was. Will I ever stop feeling so scared around him?

But I've got bigger issues to deal with than Landon. I've got only one more week with Ally. Which means that all my best friends have only one more week together to get Bluetopia going. So the two most important things right now are:

1. Friends (Ally, Chloe, and Jasper)
2. Bluetopia

Landon can wait. He has to.

B-Z Zee

2

Wink! Wink!

"I can't believe I've been in Brookdale a whole seven days," Ally said as a manicurist painted her fingernails hot pink, "and this is the first time I've been to Wink!"

"I know," Zee agreed. She was having her nails painted Sunset Splendor. "We definitely should come every day this week to make up for lost time."

"Uh-huh!" Chloe laughed. "Pedicures tomorrow. Facials Monday. Massages Tues—"

"Oh my god! I'd never ever want to go back to Paris after that!" Ally told her friends.

"There's no place like home," Zee said.

Ally pouted. "That's true."

"Aww," Chloe drawled. "Now you're making me sad."

"Luckily, there's no reason to be sad," Zee said optimistically. "Once Jasper gets Bluetopia going, we're golden. We can create an application for virtual manicures."

Chloe's eyes brightened. "That's an awesome idea! We could give everybody virtual manicures and pedicures—" she began.

"And facials and massages." Ally finished Chloe's sentence.

"Ohmylanta! That's *such* a good idea." Zee looked down at her wet fingernails. "I wish I could write it down."

"We'll remind you," Chloe said.

"I'm sure by the end of the day we'll have a ton of ideas for Bluetopia," Ally added.

"What are you guys talking about?" a familiar voice above them asked.

Zee looked up at Missy Vasi. Missy was another Brookdale Academy seventh grader. "Hey!" she greeted her. "What are you doing here?"

Missy pointed to a woman with shiny pieces of silver foil in her hair across the room. "I'm with my mom," she explained. "I just got my hair trimmed."

Zee awkwardly tugged on

the ends of her short red bob. She was a little envious of Missy's silky long hair. Missy always looked as though she'd just had her hair professionally styled. But Missy wasn't conceited about her prettiness. The girls all liked her—especially Ally, who had gotten to be friends with her on the camping trip.

"What's Bluetopia?" Missy asked.

"It's a really cool site Jasper is making," Ally explained. "It's kind of like Facebook but really small and by invitation only. I'll send you an invite."

Zee and Chloe looked at each other. "To Bluetopia?" they asked at once. Jasper had said it would be only the three of them and his British friends.

"Yeah!" Ally said excitedly.

"I don't think—" Chloe began, but Zee quickly cut her off. She didn't want to uninvite Missy.

"Uh . . . you don't think I picked the right color polish?" she said, looking at her nails. "You're right! I'll let you pick it next time."

Missy looked confused. "But it matches your awesome T-shirt," she said. She was referring to the orange shirt that Zee had silkscreened with her own tattoo-style design. Zee had changed into it when she got back from the mall so she could match the nail polish color perfectly.

Chloe looked at Zee curiously, but Zee just smiled. She was sure one more person—especially one as nice as Missy—wouldn't be a problem.

It didn't take long for a problem to appear, though. Kathi Barney walked through the door. Jen Calverez, Kathi's best friend, followed her. Kathi and Zee were not exactly friends, but most of the time they weren't enemies, either. Kathi could be really nice when she wanted to, but when it came to Zee, she rarely wanted to be. Jen usually just did what Kathi wanted her to do, so Zee couldn't count on her to be friendly—especially when Kathi was around.

"Zee! I didn't know you came here." Kathi fake-smiled and looked Zee up and down. "I thought you were more into the messy look."

Then Kathi turned to Ally. "I meant to tell you about the spa my mom and I go to whenever we're in Paris," she said brightly. "I can tell you haven't found a good place yet."

"Thanks!" Ally said. "And I can tell you—"

"Hey!" Zee interrupted, afraid of what Ally might say. She didn't want an argument to erupt in the middle of Wink. "Those are really great earrings, Jen."

Jen smiled and reached up to touch the gem hanging from her earlobe. "Thanks. Kathi gave them to me."

"I can give you the name of the boutique," Kathi said, curling her upper lip. "You know, so you don't have to keep wearing those *homemade* earrings."

"No, thanks," Zee said. "Making my jewelry is even more fun than wearing it."

"Hey, Zee, you and Landon looked like you were getting pretty friendly at the last field trip campfire," Kathi went on. "What's up with that?"

"Uh . . . I don't know," Zee said. She was pretty sure that Landon liked her, but he had been Kathi's boyfriend the year before. If competitive Kathi knew that Landon had asked Zee to hang out at the mall with him, there was no telling what she might do. Until Zee was certain about Landon, she wouldn't tell anyone but her best friends.

"Fine," Kathi said. "Don't tell me. Whatev." With a huff,

she turned to go—and came face-to-face with Mr. Papademe-triou, Brookdale Academy's instrumental music teacher.

"Mr. P?" Jen said.

Without thinking, Zee blurted out, "What are you doing here?" Mr. P was not only a music teacher, he was also the director of Zee's band, The Beans. Chloe, Kathi, Jen, Missy, Jasper, Landon, Marcus, and Conrad were all in it, too.

Mr. P ran his fingers through his tousled hair. "Well, I have to get my hair cut, too."

"It's just . . . we've never seen you here before," Jen pointed out.

Zee and Chloe nodded. "Is this your first time at Wink?" Chloe asked.

"Yup," Mr. P said.

"So what's the special occasion?" Kathi asked.

"Who said there was a special occasion?"

"Is there?" Zee coaxed.

"I know!" Jen announced. "You have a date!"

"That's it!" Ally cheered.

"Awesome!" Chloe joined in.

Mr. P's cheeks reddened. "No, that's *not* it," he protested, laughing nervously.

"It's the only thing that makes sense," Kathi told him.

Mr. P sighed, then looked from one girl to the next. "I was going to wait until Monday to tell the whole band."

"What?" the girls asked at once.

"I have a big announcement."

"What is it?" Zee wondered out loud.

"I'll tell the whole band at school."

"Wait!" Zee exclaimed. "Can't you tell us now?"

"If I told you now, that wouldn't be fair to the rest of The Beans," Mr. P said to the girls. "Plus, you wouldn't have anything to look forward to—or talk about."

"Excuse me, Mr. Papademetriou," the Wink receptionist interrupted the conversation. "Your stylist is ready for you."

Relief washed over Mr. P's face. "Now if you'll excuse me, I have to get my hair cut."

❊ ❊ ❊

When Zee and Ally got back to the Carmichaels' house, Zee logged onto her computer. She wanted to email Jasper a list of the ideas for Bluetopia that she, Chloe, and Ally had come up with at Wink.

"It would be a lot easier if Jasper were a girl," Ally said.

"Why?" Zee asked.

"Because then he would have been at Wink with us."

Zee typed in her password. "True."

"And you could talk to him about you and Landon."

"I can talk to him about me and Landon," Zee said defensively.

"Have you?" Ally asked.

"Well . . ." Zee hesitated. "No."

"That's what I thought."

"It's only because I don't think he'd be interested," Zee answered quickly. "And right now I'm not sure there's anything to say."

The computer dinged. Zee had an IM.

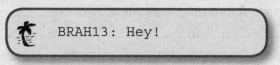

BRAH13: Hey!

"Who's Brah13?" Ally asked.

"Landon," Zee explained as a wide smile spread across her face. "It's what surfers call one another."

"Looks like he *does* like you," Ally said, plopping onto Zee's bed next to her best friend. "He's thinking about you."

 E-ZEE: Hey!

BRAH13: Wassup?

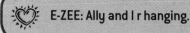 E-ZEE: Ally and I r hanging.

BRAH13: Cool.

Zee waited.

And waited.

"Say something," Ally urged.

"Like what?"

Ally thought. "Ask him what he's doing."

E-ZEE: What r u doing?

 BRAH13: Not much.

Zee waited again. Then she looked at Ally.

"Maybe he's tired," Ally suggested.

Zee shrugged. And waited. Finally, another message came.

> **BRAH13**: I downloaded a
> cool vid by Silent Noise.
> They r my favorite band.
> Do u like them?

"Ewww!" Ally said. "They're awful."

Zee knew what Ally meant. She didn't like Silent Noise, either. Not even a little. But she didn't want to insult Landon by telling him that.

As Zee thought about how to respond, an IM came from Jasper.

> **BRITCHAP**: R u there?

> **E-ZEE**: Yes.

> **BRITCHAP**: Bz afternoon.

> **E-ZEE**: 411.

> **BRITCHAP**: Dad & I went 2 a meeting.

> **E-ZEE**: What kind?

BRITCHAP: A bunch of volunteers are going to plant trees around Brookdale town hall to help fight global warming.

 E-ZEE: Cool beans!

 BRITCHAP: Then I watched Manchester City play Manchester United.

 E-ZEE: Soccer?

 BRITCHAP: Right.

 E-ZEE: Xellent.

 BRITCHAP: Then I worked on Bluetopia.

 E-ZEE: A, C & I did 2. We have ideas.

 BRITCHAP: K. Let's talk. 2mor @ my house?

 E-ZEE: K. bbfn

Bloop. A new IM came in.

BRAH13: ????

Oh no! Zee had forgotten all about Landon!

 E-ZEE: Sorry! Got another IM.

 BRAH13: K. g2g.

 E-ZEE: K. ttfn.

"That was kind of weird," Ally pointed out.

"What?" Zee asked.

"You like Landon, but you guys don't really have much to talk about, and you're just friends with Jasper, but you don't have a problem IMing at all."

Zee snorted. "That doesn't mean anything!" she said. "You and I have a lot to talk about, and we're just friends."

"I'm just saying it's too bad that you and Landon don't have more in common," Ally said, then gave Zee a curious look. "Did you think I meant that Jasper should be your boyfriend?"

"Uh . . . no," Zee said. "Why would I think that? That would be ridiculous."

"Maybe," Ally said. Then more quietly, she added, "Maybe not."

In one motion, Zee scooped up a pillow from her bed and hurled it at Ally.

"Hey!" Ally protested, but soon she started laughing. And Zee joined in.

Things I Have in Common with Landon

The Beans (Yay!)

Zee tapped her pen against her head and thought. And thought. "Oh!" she remembered.

Brookdale Academy

She thought a little more.

Friends

Most of their same friends were in The Beans, but Zee figured it still counted.

Zee looked at her list. *That's enough for now*, she decided, certain she would think of more to add to her list later.

On Sunday, Zee and Ally went over to Jasper's house to work on Bluetopia. While Zee and Jasper brainstormed ideas and designed pages, Ally read *Flip* magazine and IMed her friends in France.

"I think the background on that page is a little too dark," Zee told Jasper. "It's hard to read the letters."

"Good point," Jasper said, then moved his mouse, clicked on a few links and colors, and refreshed the page.

"Perfect!" Zee said.

"I almost forgot!" Jasper started pecking at the computer keyboard, typing a URL into his internet browser. A blue shirt came up on the screen. "Do you think I'd look good in that?" Jasper was used to wearing shirts with collars and khaki pants, but lately he was trying different things. He always got Zee's opinion before he bought something new, though.

"Yeah, it's really cool." Zee nodded.

Jasper clicked "Add to Cart" under the picture.

"I can wear it when I'm not in my school uniform."

"I thought you liked your Brookdale Academy jacket and tie so much that you slept in them," Zee teased.

Jasper shook his head. "I would *never* treat them with such disrespect," he said seriously. Then he smiled.

"Oh, you were joking!" Zee said, relieved. "For a second, I thought you were getting a little too attached to your uniform."

"Speaking of school, it's my turn to rotate the compost bin in the garden next weekend," Jasper told Zee. "Do you want to help me?"

"What do I have to do?" Zee asked.

"You just take a shovel and turn all of the leaves and vegetable scraps over," Jasper explained. "It's pretty easy if two people do it together."

Zee scrunched her nose. "Is it messy?"

"Not in the least."

"That could be fun! I'll do it." Zee looked at the computer screen, then clicked on the tab to take them back to

Bluetopia. "You know, I think that maybe we need to add some bright colors and cool graphics to the home page. It looks a little . . . boring right now."

"Do you think so?" Jasper asked. "I don't think my mates care if it's a bit drab."

"Maybe your boy mates won't, but your girl mates will." Zee looked at Ally. "Right, Ally?"

Ally lifted her eyes from her magazine. "Right, Zee."

"Show Jasper a page from the magazine," Zee suggested. Ally turned it around so Jasper could see. The page was filled with colorful jewelry, belts, and other accessories. "That's what we like," Zee told Jasper.

Jasper looked down at his hands. "Yes, it seems I need some help when it comes to understanding girls. It's good that you're here," he said quietly. He seemed shy all of a sudden.

Jasper had acted like this around other girls but never with Zee. It felt a little weird. Zee just wanted things to be normal between them.

"Without you, we wouldn't have Bluetopia at all," Zee said. "You're a computer genius. It's one of your many gifts."

Jasper flashed Zee a smile. And Zee noticed Ally spying over the top of her magazine and making a *hmm* face.

On the way back to her house, Zee was silent. She kept thinking about how well she and Jasper had worked together. And for the first time, she was really noticing how multitalented he was. Best of all, they never seemed to run out of things to say.

Do I have a crush on Jasper? Zee wondered. She shook the idea out of her head. One of the things that Zee liked best about her friendship with Jasper was that she never got a weird crushy feeling when he was around. It was just like being friends with Chloe and Ally.

Still, Zee couldn't stop wondering why she'd never told Jasper about how much she liked Landon.

Did her heart know something her head didn't?

"Oh, hello, girls!" Ginny Carmichael sang as Ally and Zee walked into the kitchen later that day. She was stirring a steaming pot on the stove.

"Hi, Mom," she said. "What's up?"

Ally sniffed the air. "Something smells delicious."

"Thanks, Ally," Zee's mother said. She picked up a handful of chopped parsley and dropped it in the pot with a flourish. "I'm making a special dinner."

"Because . . . ?" Zee prompted.

"A mother can't make a special meal for no reason?"

Zee and Ally shook their heads at the same time. "Uh-uh," they said in unison.

"Well, you'll just have to be patient," Mrs. Carmichael told them. Then she gestured toward the table. "Can you two set the places for dinner?"

Zee started putting place mats out while Ally reached into a cabinet to get glasses.

With a glass in each hand, Ally moved closer to the stove. "What are you making?"

"No peeking!" Mrs. Carmichael quickly put a lid on the pot. "You'll find out soon enough. When you girls are finished with the table, why don't you occupy yourselves until the meal's ready?" She began whistling as she chopped onions.

"I know when I'm not wanted," Zee said.

As Zee folded a cloth

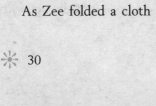

napkin on each place mat, Ally came behind and put a fork on top. "Let's go play Wii," she suggested when they were done, then headed out of the kitchen.

Zee followed. "Okay," she agreed.

In the TV room, Ally grabbed a game control and sank into the Carmichaels' couch. "A lot of people are keeping secrets around here," she said.

"Who?" Zee asked. "Me?"

Ally studied Zee. "I don't know. Are you?"

"Uh . . . no. I just thought you thought I was," Zee said quickly. "But of course I'm not. Why would I? . . . I'll stop rambling now."

"I just meant your mom and Mr. P," Ally explained.

"Oh yeah. Them." Zee sat down next to Ally.

"Maybe it's the same secret," Ally suggested. "We might find out before everyone else."

"What could it be?" Zee wondered out loud.

Ally thought. "The Beans could be going on tour."

Zee shook her head. "It's too soon for the band. We all have to go to school."

"I guess you're right," Ally agreed. "Plus, that doesn't explain your mother's weird mood."

"It is weird, isn't it?" Zee asked. "I mean, she loves cooking, and she's almost always in a good mood, but this is a little *too* good. She never whistles."

"Maybe we're twin sisters who were separated at birth," Ally suggested.

Zee studied her friend skeptically. The girls were both wearing tank tops and shorts rolled up to make cuffs, but that was where the similarities ended. Zee had a face full of freckles and a short red bob. There wasn't a single freckle on Ally's face, and her smooth, thick brown hair reached halfway down her back.

"I think we need another theory," Zee said.

"What else could it be?"

"Okeydokey!" Mrs. Carmichael cooed from the doorway. "Dinner's ready!"

"We'll find out soon," Zee said, leading Ally to the kitchen.

Mr. Carmichael was lighting a candle.

"Fancy," Adam said, taking his seat at the table. "What's up?"

"It's a special night," Mrs. Carmichael said, sitting down next to her son.

Ally pointed at herself, then Zee, and mouthed, "Twins."

"What did you say?" Mrs. Carmichael said, surprised.

"Oh, nothing important," Ally said quickly.

Adam looked at his mother. "Did you finally sign up Zee for the circus—" he began, "as the monkey?"

"That's funny," Zee said. "Not."

"Good comeback," Adam responded. "Not."

"All right, you two," Mr. Carmichael cut in. "Stop teasing each other." Instead of looking upset with his kids, though, a smile stretched across his face.

"I feel like I'm living in the twilight zone," Zee groaned. "Would someone please tell me what you're talking about?"

"We won't keep you in suspense any longer." Zee's mother reached over and grabbed her father's hand. Then she looked at him with what could only be described as goo-goo eyes. Yuck! "We're expecting," she said.

Zee, Adam, and Ally all leaned forward.

"A delivery?" Zee asked.

"Yes!" Mr. Carmichael said.

"Of what?" Ally asked.

"Babies!" Mrs. Carmichael said.

"Whose?" Adam asked, confused.

"Ours," his mother told him. "Yours."

"Ummm . . . Mom? I'm going to need a do-over, because I don't get it," Zee said.

"Your mother is pregnant," Zee's father explained.

Zee's mouth dropped open as the news sunk in. The feelings inside Zee morphed from joy to confusion to shock.

Adam started laughing. "Good one!" he said. "Very funny. You almost had me going."

Mrs. Carmichael looked confused. "It's not a joke."

When she could finally speak, Zee said, "But you said 'babies.' As in *plural*. As in *many*."

Zee's father laughed. "Just two."

"Two *babies*?" Zee asked.

"Twins."

"I knew it had something to do with twins!" Ally shouted triumphantly. "How awesome is that?"

"Cool beans!" Zee said. "I'm going to make them some amazing clothes. Boys or girls?"

"Or girl *and* boy?" Ally asked.

Zee's mother laughed. "We don't know. We've decided to be surprised."

"I love surprises," Zee said.

"Me too," Ally agreed. "I want to be here when they're born."

"That would be incredible!" Zee said. "After all, they'll practically be your sisters—or brothers—too."

"Well, I'm glad I'm going to college. I'll be leaving just in time," Adam said.

"What do you mean?" Zee asked.

"I'll escape the screaming and crying."

"I'm sure the babies won't be so bad," Zee's father told him.

"I wasn't talking about the babies," Adam explained. "I was talking about Zee."

"Why would I be screaming and crying?" Zee asked.

"You're not going to be the youngest anymore. I bet you'll be whinier than the twins."

"Oh, that's silly," Mrs. Carmichael said. "Look at how excited she is."

A knot tightened in Zee's stomach. "Uh . . . yeah." She stumbled on her words. "Totally."

Lost in her thoughts, Zee didn't hear much of what the others said after that. *Is Adam actually right?* she wondered. Zee had liked the idea that she'd be an only child when Adam was away at college. She'd have the house—and her parents—to herself. Now she'd have to share with *two* babies.

Zee was going to be outnumbered! She had to tell Chloe the news.

 E-ZEE: U r not going 2 believe this!

 SOCCERNOW: What?

 E-ZEE: My mom is going 2 have twins.

SOCCERNOW: Awesome!!!

 E-ZEE: Do u think so?

 SOCCERNOW: R u kidding??!! I don't have any bros or sisters. U will have 3. U r soooooo lucky!

 E-ZEE: I didn't think of it that way. I guess u r right!

After Zee logged off, she opened up her diary.

Hi, Diary,

Chloe made me feel tons better. I will never ever tell Adam this, but I'm going to miss him when he's at college. The babies will keep me from being too lonely. Now I'm really excited about ~~it~~ them.

I still have a problem, though. Landon. It used to be that my problem was that I liked him, but he didn't like me back. Now I'm worried he might actually like me and we'll never have anything to say!

Which leads to Problem, Part Two. Jasper. What if I like him? How can you tell a friend from a crush?

Zee

4

More News

"I think they should have made you wear your uniform from last year," Zee said to Ally as she tugged the collar of her school-issued white shirt. The girls were walking to instrumental music class the next morning. First period was when The Beans rehearsed.

"That uniform's too small for me now," Ally told her. "Besides, those things are awful. Why would you want me to suffer?"

"I guess misery loves company."

Ally put her hand on Zee's shoulder. "I didn't mean you look awful." She pointed to the necklace Zee was wearing. Zee had rolled magazine paper into beads and strung them together. "You always make the uniform look cool with your jewelry and tights and Converse."

"Thanks!" Zee smiled. Then she added, "I'll make you a necklace, too."

"Awesome!"

"Hey, guys!" Chloe's southern accent rang out behind Zee and Ally. They waited for their friend to catch up. "Do you have any idea what Mr. P's big announcement is?" Chloe asked as she got closer to her friends.

"Ohmylanta!" Zee said. "I completely forgot."

"Maybe he's getting married," Ally suggested as the group rounded the corner toward the music classroom.

Zee shook her head. "I don't think he even has a girl-friend."

"What do you think it is, Chloe?" Ally asked.

"Heck if I know," Chloe said.

"Maybe The Beans are getting a new band member," Ally suggested.

"That might be fun," Chloe said.

"I don't know," Zee said. "It might get a little too crowded."

"I say, the more, the merrier," Chloe replied, bounding through the classroom door in front of her friends.

As Zee walked into the room, she noticed Mr. P by the whiteboard. Instead of leaning against his desk the way he usually did, he stood up straight. He was more dressed up than usual. His white dress shirt and black pants were wrinkle-free, he had trimmed the little patch of beard that grew between his lip and chin, and his new haircut topped off the look.

"What's with him?" Ally whispered as she and Zee took their seats next to Chloe.

Zee shrugged. "I'm not sure."

"At first, I thought we had a substitute," Chloe said. "I didn't recognize him at all."

"Looking sharp, Mr. P," Conrad shouted as he made his way to a chair next to the piano. "Did you get dressed up for any special reason?"

Mr. P's face reddened. "Uh . . . no," he stammered. "Just my students."

"Hey! You mean we're not special?" Conrad protested.

Mr. P nervously ran his fingers through his hair. "Of course. I just mean, today's not different from any other day." He paused. "Sort of."

Ally turned to Zee and Chloe. "Sort of?" she whispered. "What do you think that means?"

"Why would he need to get so dressed up just for an announcement?" Zee asked.

"My dad says he can always tell who is going on a job interview at his office," Chloe said. "They dress nicer than usual."

"You think Mr. P has a job interview?" Ally asked.

"I don't think he'd leave us," Zee said, then looked around. "Speaking of which . . . where's Jasper?"

"He said he had to go to the technology lab to ask Ms. Short a question about programming Bluetopia," Chloe explained. "He should be back soon."

"Why are you looking for Jasper?" Ally asked.

"I just don't want him to be marked tardy," Zee said. "Why else?"

"Uh . . . no reason," Ally said. "Just wondering why it mattered."

"He should be here for Mr. P's announcement."

Zee breathed a sigh of relief as the first-period bell rang and Jasper came through the door and slid into his seat.

"Great!" Mr. P said. "Let's get started."

"Aren't you going to take attendance?" Jen asked.

"If you're not here, raise your hand!" Conrad joked. Mr. P and the rest of the class laughed.

"I kept track as everyone came in. The Beans are all here. Which is good, because I have something important to tell you." He rubbed his hands together. "The school is so happy with The Beans that it wants to see if we can re-create that success in some of the other music classes in the upper grades. I now have additional teaching responsibilities."

Zee panicked. "You're leaving us?" she blurted out.

"Never," Mr. P assured her, then looked at the others. "But I will need help with The Beans in order for things to keep running smoothly."

"What kind of help?" Chloe asked.

"Brookdale Academy has hired an assistant teacher for this class," Mr. P began, then glanced at the door. "Please come in," he called.

A thin woman with wavy brown hair and a gray scarf tied around her long neck walked into the room.

Kathi gasped. Zee nearly did, too. The new teacher looked more like a movie star. She wore an elegant gray suit, but instead of buttons, the front of the jacket scooped down and tied off to the side with two thin strings. As she moved across the room, her pants accented her graceful movements.

The room hummed with excited murmurs.

"I'm pleased to introduce Ms. Vardolis," Mr. P said, settling everyone down. "Not only is she an accomplished classical pianist, but she has also toured the world with the Los Angeles Ballet."

"Wow!" Zee said to her friends. "A musician *and* a dancer." She knew that no one could replace Mr. P, but it would be great to have someone who could help The Beans with their choreography as well as the music.

"This is going to be so awesome," Chloe said.

From the smiles and buzz of whispers, everyone seemed thrilled about the idea. Except Kathi. She slouched in her seat with her arms crossed.

"What's with her?" Ally asked.

"I think she's upset she didn't get an award," Zee explained.

"It would be cool if everyone introduced themselves and if each of you told Ms. Vardolis what instrument you play," suggested Mr. P. "Let's start with you, Jasper."

Jasper cleared his throat. "Hello, I'm Jasper Chapman, and I play bass."

"It's very nice to meet you, Jasper," Ms. Vardolis said in a soft voice.

Next came Missy. Then Conrad and Marcus.

When it was Landon's turn he said, "Landon Beck," then hit his drums with a *ba-dum-bum*. Conrad and Marcus high-fived him.

"I'm Ally Stern," Ally said when it was her turn. "And I'm not actually a Brookdale student, but I am an honorary Bean. I play the flute."

Ms. Vardolis looked confused. "You're not a student?"

"No. I used to be, but now I live in France. I'm just visiting."

"Ah, bonjour, Ally," Ms. Vardolis said. Then she said something in French that sounded completely amazing.

Since Zee had just started taking French this year, she had no idea what it was.

"*Oui,*" Ally responded, nodding.

Zee was next. "Hi, I'm Mackenzie Blue, and I play the guitar, and your French is ten times better than mine."

"Well, I went to school there for four years, so I've had a lot of practice," Ms. Vardolis said.

"Wow!" Chloe said. "Do you know any other languages?"

"I'll tell you if you tell me your name," Ms. Vardolis said with a smile.

"Oh, sorry. I'm Chloe, and I play the cello."

"I also speak Spanish, Italian, Russian, and a little German."

Kathi grunted, but Zee couldn't tell if the new teacher heard it or not. Ms. Vardolis just turned to Jen and looked at her expectantly.

After Jen finished, it was finally Kathi's turn.

"Hello, Kathi," Ms. Vardolis said.

How does she know Kathi's name? Zee wondered.

"Hi, Roxy," Kathi sulked.

Roxy? Zee said to herself. Was that Ms. Vardolis's first name?

All of the students stared at the two of them.

45

Ms. Vardolis broke the silence with a chuckle. "I bet you're wondering how Kathi and I know each other."

A few students nodded.

"Kathi and I are cousins," Ms. Vardolis went on. "Our mothers are sisters. Since I'm older than Kathi and spent a great deal of my life touring the world, I didn't get a chance to spend much time in Brookdale with her. I'm so thrilled to be able to do that now."

Kathi didn't look quite so happy about it. She plastered a fake grin on her face and said, "Yes. How nice."

"At least she's being polite," Ally whispered, and Chloe nodded.

Still, Zee thought. *Why doesn't Kathi like Ms. Vardolis?* She seemed so great.

"Ms. Vardolis came at just the right time," Mr. P said, breaking into Zee's thoughts. "I got news this weekend that The Beans have been chosen to be one of the featured bands at Brookdale Day."

"Our first real concert!" Zee shouted, throwing her arms over her head. She quickly pulled her hand to her lips. "Oops! Sorry."

"Isn't that on Saturday?" Chloe asked.

"Yes," Mr. P said.

"How are we going to be ready by Saturday?" Kathi asked.

"We can do it!" Jen told her.

"That's the spirit! You've been practicing together for a while now," Mr. P pointed out. "You just need to make it happen—just like a professional band would."

A professional band. Mr. P's words echoed in Zee's head as she started to smile. She was moving one step closer to her dream of becoming a professional rock star.

At lunch that day, Zee was eager to share her latest Bluetopia ideas with Jasper. "I was thinking that everyone on Bluetopia could have a notebook," she explained. "And the messages that people post to one another could be called doodles."

Jasper's eyes lit up. "Brilliant!" he said. "I would have just called them something daft like posts."

"Also, I think we have to have a fashion application," Zee went on.

Ally turned to Zee. "I *love* that idea," she agreed. "We could design our own clothes and trade them with our friends."

"I'm not sure my mates in London would really feel the need to trade clothes," Jasper pointed out.

"Well, I know your mates in Brookdale would," Ally told him. "All that soccer stuff you're planning is fine, but we need something interesting for us."

Chloe, who was sitting next to Jasper, swallowed her falafel sandwich. "I love soccer—and I love fashion, too."

"So that's three votes for fashion," Ally said.

"I'll see what I can do," Jasper gave in.

"Cool beans!" Zee cheered.

"Awesome!" added Chloe.

"What's so awesome?" Landon asked, placing his tray in the empty space next to Zee.

The smile on Jasper's face disappeared as Landon slid into the seat. "Uh . . .

um . . ." As hard as she tried, Zee could not remember what they had just been talking about. Seeing Landon and Jasper together made her head spin.

Ally went in for the save. "Fashion."

"Not interesting," Landon said, then looked at Jasper. "Right, bro?"

Zee was happy to have Landon nearby, but she was also nervous. For some reason, Jasper and Landon didn't always get along.

"I don't have a choice except to think it's quite brilliant," Jasper explained. "It's three against one."

"That's your problem," Landon said before he took a bite of apple.

"Yes, it would seem so."

They're talking, Zee thought. *Like they're friends.* She smiled, relieved that she could sit next to Landon and not worry about Jasper.

Marcus and Conrad sat down next to Landon.

"I hope we'll be ready for the concert by Saturday," Zee told the group.

"I'm not worried," Conrad said.

"Really?" Chloe asked. "Why not?"

"Well, I don't know about you guys, but I plan to be awesome—as usual," Conrad explained.

Ally rolled her eyes. "What about you, Marcus?" she asked.

"Oh, I'm pretty awesome, too," Marcus told her.

Zee noticed Chloe's cheeks redden slightly as she giggled at Marcus's joke.

"Luckily, Ms. Vardolis is here to help us," Zee reminded the table.

"Having Roxy as a teacher is *the worst* thing that has ever happened to me in my *whole* life!" Kathi declared as she walked up with Jen.

"I've never seen you this upset," Jen told her.

"Why don't you like her?" Zee asked Kathi.

"Isn't it obvious?" Kathi responded.

Everyone except Kathi shook his or her head. Even Jen looked confused.

Kathi gave an exasperated sigh. "Roxy is a show-off."

"Really?" Zee asked.

Kathi nodded. "Well, at least her mother is. Aunt Nancy is always calling my mother to tell her all of the fabulous stuff Roxy has done."

"Maybe you're just jealous," Chloe said.

Jen flinched at the remark.

Kathi glared at Chloe. "Hardly," she said. "It wouldn't bother me if my mother didn't care so much. Every time she gets off the phone with Aunt Nancy, she reminds me that I'm not half as accomplished as Roxy."

Jen nodded. "It's pretty bad."

"Well," Zee began, starting to feel sorry for Kathi, "Roxy is at least ten years older."

"But she's been winning awards and getting the starring roles her whole life—or at least my whole life."

"Still, it's not Roxy's fault if your mother makes you feel bad," Zee continued.

Kathi crossed her arms. "Yes, it is!" she said. "If she weren't so perfect, her mother wouldn't have anything to brag about."

"Maybe this is your chance to show Roxy that you're just as good as she is," Jen suggested.

Kathi looked at Jen. Her angry face softened. "You're right!" Kathi said, beaming. "But how?"

Before Jen could answer, Missy rushed over to the group and took the seat next to Ally. "Ugh!" she complained. "My dad accidentally gave me Zane's lunch, so I had to go all the way over to the other school building to trade with him." Zane was one of Missy's younger twin brothers. "That's a long walk when you're hungry."

"Oh my gosh, Zee!" Ally exclaimed. "I just realized you're going to have something in common with Missy."

"What?" Missy asked, looking at Zee.

Everyone turned toward Zee. But Zee couldn't figure out what Ally was talking about.

"Twins!" Ally said.

"Ohmylanta!" Zee said. "I totally forgot. My mom is pregnant."

"Pregnant?" Kathi asked. "Isn't she a little old?"

Zee shrugged. "I guess not."

"She probably just wanted another chance to get it right," Kathi added.

"Get what right?" Chloe asked.

Kathi looked Zee up and down. "You know, kids."

This time, Missy made the save. "Awesome, Zee."

"What is being the older sister to twins like?" Zee asked.

"Well . . . ," Missy began. "We call them Double Trouble."

"Trouble?" Zee repeated.

"My dad came up with the nickname when they were babies," Missy explained. "Zane would finally stop crying, then Steven would start."

"Oh," Zee said, getting worried.

"And then as soon as my parents finally got Steven to take a nap, Zane would wake up from his," Missy said. "Then he'd cry."

"They're not babies anymore," Zee pointed out. "So it must be better. Right?" she asked hopefully.

Missy shrugged. "A little. But my parents still joke that if they had known how hard twins would be, they would have gotten a twin set of parents. Sometimes I wish I had a clone when they want me to play with them."

Zee looked down at her lunch. "Hmm."

"And I still have to work twice as hard to get my parents to notice me," Missy went on.

Zee gulped—even though she hadn't taken a bite of food since Missy had sat down.

Hi, Diary,
You've got to help me figure out if I'm better off with or without twins in my life.

Ways My Life Is Going to Change	Ways My Life Is Going to Be the Same
I'm going to be the middle child.	Ally, Chloe, and Jasper will always be my best friends.
I'll have to share my parents even more.	I'll be a Brookdale student.
I'll have to share everything even more.	
The house will be noisy.	
I'll have to babysit.	

Zee studied the uneven columns on her list. There was so much in her life that was going to be different.

> Did my parents even think about how it would affect other people when they decided to have another baby (or two)?
>
> Zee

5

Bluetopia Live!

While Zee worked on her math homework in her bedroom after school, Ally sat next to her on the bed. She was typing an email to Jacques, her boyfriend in France, on Zee's laptop.

Ding! went the computer.

"It's an email from Jasper!" Ally announced. "Bluetopia is online!"

Happy to take a break, Zee dropped her pencil and read the message that Jasper had also sent to Chloe and all his friends in England.

Bluetopia has officially launched! Register and log on to let everyone know what you're doing and to find out what your buds are up to.

"Hey, look!" Zee said, pointing at the screen. "He took my suggestion."

"Which one?" Ally asked.

"He wanted to call your friends who join 'mates,' but I told him 'mates' was too stuffy and he should use 'buds' instead."

Ally clicked on the link at the bottom of the email.

The home page was a swirl of bold reds, oranges, and blues. An animated flower opened and closed, and a soccer player kicked a ball into a goal.

"Cool beans!" Zee exclaimed. "It looks even better than I expected."

Ally clicked on the "Register" link. "I can't wait to make you, Chloe, and Jasper my friends," Ally said as she typed.

"Don't you mean buds?" Zee asked and giggled.

"This is going to be awesome!" Ally finished registering then slid the computer to Zee. "Your turn."

Zee began to type in her name, then paused. "Maybe Jasper, you, Chloe, and I should test Bluetopia before it goes all the way across the ocean to London. What if there are glitches in the program?"

"But he sent the email to everyone," Ally pointed out.

"They're probably all asleep because of the time

difference between here and there. Jasper could send another email telling them to wait a few days."

As the girls talked, Zee got an IM.

 BRITCHAP: Did u get my email?

 E-ZEE: Yes, A already registered.
I m going 2 now.

Zee told him about her idea to test the site with the Brookdale group first.

 BRITCHAP: We need more people 4 a real test. Anyway there aren't ever going 2 b many people. I can fix the probs in a jiff and get everything back and running fast.

E-ZEE: U r right. I probably worry 2 much.

 BRITCHAP: C u in Bluetopia!

At that moment, Zee's mother walked into the room with a tape measure.

"What's that for?" Zee asked.

"I was wondering if you might want to move to the guest room at the end of the hall."

Zee looked around at her peach walls decorated with an autographed Jonas Brothers poster, her cozy, overstuffed chair, and her white four-poster bed. "Why?"

"This room is so much closer to the master bedroom," Mrs. Carmichael pointed out. "So when the babies cry in the middle of the night, we'll be able to get in here faster to take care of them."

Zee thought about her mother's explanation and had to admit it made sense.

"That would be so awesome! The guest room is *huge*, and you'll be able to decorate it however you want," Ally chimed in. She looked around. "This is like your kid room, and your new room will be your teenager room."

Zee knew Ally was right. It could be a lot of fun to start over completely. Still, Zee had been in her bedroom since she was a baby—and she wasn't ready to give it up.

"Umm . . . I'll think about it."

"Thanks!" her mother said, taking the tape measure with her as she walked out.

Zee went back onto Bluetopia. By now, Chloe had logged on and sent Zee a pedicure. Zee began to search through

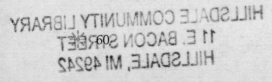

the fashion application, looking for the perfect outfit to send her friend.

But Zee was having trouble focusing on the choices. She couldn't get her conversation with her mother out of her head. *Are Mom and Dad going to kick me out of my room?* she wondered.

As Zee clicked around the site, the word *blog* jumped off the screen. *That's it!* she thought. Ally was right. She was going to be a teenager soon. Maybe she should welcome all the changes. *I can turn my diary into a private blog.* This way, there was no chance anyone would see it.

Zee clicked on the box labeled "Private View" and began her first entry.

> Hi, Bloggo,
> My parents are trying to get me out of the way already. My mom didn't say I *have* to move down the hall, but I know that's what she really wants. It's weird to think about all of the changes that are going to happen now that the babies are coming. Is Missy right? Am I going to have to work twice as hard to get my parents' attention? And if I don't, are they going to forget about me?
> Zee

"What are you doing?" Ally asked.

Zee quickly closed the screen. "I was trying to find an outfit from the fashion application to send to Chloe."

"We should start a Fashionista Club and invite her to join it," Ally said.

"Cool beans!" Zee agreed. "We can talk about the clothes or jewelry we just bought or made."

"And let everyone know about any awesome sales," Ally suggested.

"And post pictures of what celebrities are wearing, and everyone can rate them," Zee added. She'd rather talk about fashion with Ally than think about all of her problems.

Zee sent an invitation to Chloe to join the club, and doodled a message in the club notebook. "For girls who love—and live—fashion. Spot the hottest trends and post about them here."

"Bluetopia's going to be even better than I thought," Ally said.

The girls began sending gifts, messages, bunnies, gems, and jokes to one another and their friends. They made

doodles in each other's notebooks as well as in Chloe's and Jasper's.

Then Ally clicked on the "Invite a Bud" link.

"Who are you inviting?" Zee asked.

"Missy," Ally answered without looking up from the screen. "Remember? I promised."

"Oh yeah," Zee said, a little worried. Then she realized that having Missy on Bluetopia might not be such a bad idea. It would be nice to have a bud who understood what it was like to be the older sister of twins—the good and the bad parts.

"Girls!" Mr. Carmichael called up the stairs. "Dinner is in five minutes. Please come down and set the table."

"Just a second," Zee called back. Then she said to Ally, "I'm just going to send Jasper a thank-you gift for making Bluetopia."

"I'll start setting the table," Ally said.

As Ally headed to the door, Zee sent Jasper a red rose. Almost immediately, he sent one back. And her heart began to pound—just like it used to when Landon was near her. But this was her good friend Jasper! Zee was confused.

It was time for another blog entry.

Hi, Bloggoni,

Did you miss me? JK.

Can I have a crush on my friend? I've always thought of Jasper as my boy friend, not my boyfriend. Now something feels totally different. I mean, from the time I met him, I thought he was great. He's super-talented and he really cares about the environment. He's also funny (even though I don't think he's always trying to be). And he has an awesome accent. But all that stuff describes Chloe, too. So what's the difference? It all started with Bluetopia. But Bluetopia is not real. Sort of. I mean, it's a virtual world. Gifts aren't real. Money isn't real. I'm worried that I just like him because he created this really cool website. Maybe it's not a real crush, either.

Zee

"Zee!" Ally called from downstairs. "Dinner!"

"Coming!" Zee shouted back. She shut down her computer and hurried out of her room.

6

Bluetopia Blowup!

"Look!" Zee shouted as she and Ally got out of Adam's red subcompact before school on Tuesday morning. "There are Chloe and Jasper." She pointed across the Brookdale Academy parking lot.

"Hey! Wait for us!" Ally called out to their best friends, then hurried over.

"Did you get the hug I sent you this morning?" Zee asked Chloe.

"Yes!" Chloe told her, then pointed to Zee's black skateboarding Converse with the bright purple laces. "I knew you were going to wear those sneakers."

"How?" Zee asked.

"You posted a photo in the Fashionista Club."

Zee giggled. "I forgot."

"Did you see that all my mates from London are on, too?" Jasper asked.

"I was talking soccer with most of them during breakfast this morning," Chloe told him.

"Someone named Colin even joined the Fashionista Club!" Ally added.

"Colin is quite a smart dresser," Jasper said. Then he got a serious look on his face. "I was surprised to see Missy on Bluetopia. Who invited her?"

"I did," Ally explained. "She heard us talking about it, and I didn't want to be rude and leave her out."

When Jasper frowned, Zee was glad she had followed his rules. She didn't want him to be upset with her. Still, she had to admit she hadn't tried very hard to stop Ally.

"Ally didn't think it would be a problem," Zee defended her friend. "And Missy is so nice and cool."

Jasper's expression softened.

"I'm sorry, Jasper," Ally apologized, then spotted Missy passing one of the rain barrels that surrounded the school. "I'll tell her not to invite any more people."

Missy gave the group a big wave, then hurried to them. "I started a Pets Club and invited all you guys to join," she announced.

"Um . . . that's great," Ally said. "But just be sure to keep Bluetopia private with us. There can't be any more members."

"Oh no!" Missy's bright smile disappeared. "I didn't know I wasn't supposed to invite other people."

"Who did you invite?" Jasper asked.

"Just Conrad and Marcus," Missy quickly explained.

"Okay," Jasper said. "But that's it." He looked at each of the girls.

"Definitely," Missy assured him and then everyone else nodded.

Brrrrng! The bell rang overhead.

"We'd better go," Zee said. "First period's going to start." They headed into the building and down the main hallway.

When the group entered the music classroom, Zee noticed Landon punching the buttons on his telephone keyboard. *This is my chance*, she thought. She was determined to have a normal conversation with him without feeling completely weird.

"Hi," Zee said.

"Oh, hey!" Landon said, looking up.

"What are you doing?" Zee asked.

"I'm talking to some English dude on Bluetopia."

"You know about Bluetopia?"

"Yeah. Marcus invited me."

Jasper overheard the conversation as he passed by to get to his seat. "It wasn't really intended for surfer dudes," he mumbled to himself.

Kathi and Jen walked into the room just as the late bell rang.

"Hey!" Landon called to them. "Did you get my invitation for Bluetopia?"

Please say no. Please say no, Zee silently pleaded.

"Yeah!" Kathi said. "Thanks!"

Zee's heart dropped right into her Converse. How could Landon do this to her? Bluetopia was supposed to be for just a few close friends. It should have been a place where she wouldn't have to worry about Kathi. But she'd found her way in.

"All right, students!" Ms. Vardolis called out. "Take your seats and we will begin."

Zee turned to Jasper and gave a weak smile. Things were not working out the way they had planned.

7
The Assistant's Assistant

"$\mathcal{M}$r. P is in a meeting with the head of school, Dr. Harrison, so I will be diving right in," Ms. Vardolis announced after The Beans had settled into their seats. Zee couldn't help but notice how Ms. Vardolis's smooth voice seemed to match her silk clothes.

"We have a lot to accomplish before Saturday," the assistant teacher continued. "You'll be performing a couple of new songs as well as a few you've been practicing already."

"New songs?" Conrad blurted out, surprised.

"Oh, fab," Kathi mumbled sarcastically. Then she looked at Ms. Vardolis. "I mean, no prob," she said louder. Was Kathi actually following Jen's advice and trying to impress her cousin?

Ohmylanta, Zee groaned to herself as her heart began to beat a little faster. It wouldn't be easy to learn all the new music in less than a week.

"Mr. P and I know that you won't have any problem with the new material," Ms. Vardolis assured the class. Her vote of confidence immediately calmed Zee's pounding heart. "In fact, one of you probably knows a couple of the songs quite well," she said as she began handing out the band's playlist for Brookdale Day.

"Hey, Zee!" Chloe shouted. "You wrote two of these songs."

"Really?" Zee asked, looking at the sheet of paper. Two of her songs—"Solve It" and "My Heart"— jumped off the page. "Cool beans!" she said.

Kathi snorted.

Ms. Vardolis looked at Zee. "I couldn't believe it when Mr. P told me that a seventh grader had written these songs. We both agreed that the world should hear them."

The world? Zee repeated silently. Her face felt warm, and she was sure her cheeks were bright red from embarrassment.

"Why don't we start by practicing Mackenzie's songs first?" Ms. Vardolis passed out the sheet music for "Solve It." "Because we have so little time to prepare, I arranged the songs myself," she said, looking at Zee. "I hope that's okay."

Zee wanted to say, "It's more than okay. It's incredible that you would want to arrange my songs." But she was too tongue-tied to say anything besides, "Uh . . . that's . . . fine."

"I can't believe it! There's a marimba solo," Jen enthused. She smiled at Zee.

"And a drum solo," Landon added.

Kathi's hand shot up in the air. "You arranged this for me to sing backup, but I can sing lead, too."

"That's very nice of you, Kathi," her cousin told her. "But I think it makes more sense for Mackenzie to sing lead since she already knows the words. That's less you need to learn." Kathi slumped in her chair and frowned as Ms. Vardolis turned to Zee. "And since you know the songs so well, Mackenzie, how would you like to be the assistant teacher's assistant?"

"Cool beans!" Zee blurted out. It would be amazing to work alongside someone who had so much professional experience.

Ms. Vardolis flicked her hand. "Come up to the front

of the room, then, and we'll get started." The rest of The Beans got ready to begin playing music.

Ms. Vardolis directed the group, and Zee played along with the others. Then the teacher stopped the band and turned to Zee. "Do you think we should have less bass there?"

Zee pointed to herself. "Are you asking *me*?" she said.

Ms. Vardolis smiled. "Yes, I am."

"I don't think so," Zee said, then added, "but maybe the piano could play harmony."

"You're right! That would give this part a much richer sound. I'll fix the arrangement," Ms. Vardolis said. "Please start at the beginning."

"Uhh . . . what should I do while you fix my part?" Marcus asked. He was the band's pianist.

Ms. Vardolis turned to Zee. "What do you think?"

"Um . . . why don't you play the major chords when you get to that part?" Zee suggested.

"Good idea." Ms. Vardolis smiled. As she stepped toward her desk, Zee counted out the beat, and The Beans began to play again.

The rest of the rehearsal went very well. The Beans worked hard to get their parts right. Kathi was cooperating, too, which was a huge surprise. Even though Kathi had said she was going to try to impress her cousin, Zee couldn't help but wonder if Kathi might be secretly plotting revenge—against her.

"It is so unbelievably cool that I am going to be in The Beans' first big concert!" Ally said excitedly as she, Zee, Jasper, Chloe, and Missy walked to the Carmichaels' house after school. "When The Beans become an international success, I can play with you when you're in France."

"We'll be a worldwide sensation by Saturday afternoon," Jasper commented.

"We will?" Missy asked.

"As soon as we post a video of the show on Bluetopia, Jasper's friends in London will see us," Zee explained.

"You read my mind!" Jasper told her.

"Great minds think alike!" Zee put in, giving Jasper a nudge with her elbow. She quickly pulled it away. *Why did I do that?* she asked herself. She and Jasper had kidded around with jabs and jokes since they'd met. Why was this time different?

"Jasper, you should create a Bluetopia page for The Beans." Chloe interrupted Zee's thoughts. "We can have all of The Beans join."

"Brilliant!" Jasper agreed. "We can post updates and stuff about Brookdale Day. That will keep the planning very organized."

Zee pushed open the front door to her home, and her friends followed her inside. Jasper led the charge into the kitchen, where Zee expected to find her mother—and the usual plate of delicious homemade snacks.

Jasper looked around frantically. "Where are the garlic pita toasts? Where's the black bean dip?"

"Where's my mother?" Zee asked.

"Is she gone, Zee?" Chloe asked. "Because I can't be here without an adult."

"Maybe she went to the grocery store to get some snack ingredients," Jasper suggested, licking his lips.

Zee looked at her iPhone and shook her head. "Mom must be here," she told her friends. "She didn't text me and the front door was unlocked." With her friends right behind her, Zee moved from the kitchen to the TV room, through the dining room, and into the living room. Then she peeked into the laundry room and knocked on the powder room door. No sign of her mother.

"Maybe she's upstairs," Missy said.

"I'll check," Zee said, zooming up the flight of steps as quickly as she could.

Picturing her mother buried underneath a pile of her brother's dirty clothes, Zee headed straight for Adam's room. When she looked in, her mother wasn't anywhere. "Mom?" she called out just in case. But there was no response.

Then Zee remembered her parents' plan to turn her room into a nursery. She hurried to her bedroom, half-expecting to see her mother painting the walls. Mrs. Carmichael wasn't there, either.

Zee glanced across the hallway through her parents' open door. Her mother's body was stretched across the bed, her head sunk deep in a pillow.

Zee stepped into the room. "Mom," Zee whispered. But her mother didn't move. Instead she snored softly. "Mom." Zee's voice got louder—but not loud enough to wake her mother. "Mom!" Zee barked.

"What is it?" Mrs. Carmichael asked groggily.

"I'm home from school. My friends are here, too. Remember? I told you we were all going to walk home together today."

"Oh, of course, I remember," Zee's mom said, and Zee was relieved that she had not been completely forgotten.

"I just came up for a little rest, and I must have fallen asleep," Mrs. Carmichael told Zee. "I guess this pregnancy is really wearing me out. My body isn't used to taking care of two other people." She laughed as she sat up, but Zee didn't feel like laughing. She hadn't realized how tired her mother would be *before* the twins were even born.

"Are you going to come downstairs?" Zee asked.

"Of course, sweetie," her mother said. "Just let me put myself together. You and your friends can grab snacks from the cabinet."

Snacks from the cabinet? Zee couldn't believe her ears! Usually, all the prepackaged food was off-limits.

When Zee got back downstairs, her friends were gathered around the Wii, playing baseball.

"Was Ginny up there?" Ally asked Zee.

"She was taking a nap," Zee told her friends.

"A nap?" Chloe said. "I didn't know she *ever* slept."

"I'm relieved," Jasper said without taking his eyes off the video screen. "I thought she'd taken off with the snacks, never to be seen again."

"Well . . . she's here, but the snacks aren't," Zee explained. "She didn't get a chance to make anything today."

In shock, Jasper spun his head around to look at Zee. He struck out in the game. "Oh, bother!" he said. "I'm so upset, I can't even concentrate on baseball."

"Sorry, guys," Zee apologized.

Missy shrugged. "It's not a big deal. Your mom's snacks are fun and all, but that's not why we came over."

Ally popped up out of her seat. "Let's see what's in the cabinet."

Jasper put down his game control and went into the kitchen with the others. They pulled out rice cakes, almond butter, cheese, and crackers.

"Aaah, a fine snack indeed," Jasper said, rubbing his belly.

"I guess," Zee said. She knew that she was feeling badly not because of the food but about the fact that her mother had forgotten her and her friends.

"It must be really weird to have two bodies growing inside of you," Ally said as she smeared almond butter on a rice cake. "Like aliens."

"My mom says that when she was pregnant she used to look down and see her stomach moving around! My dad called it the Baby Channel," Chloe told her.

"Definitely alien forces at work," Ally said matter-of-factly.

The friends laughed, but Zee was still worried.

"Was your mother always tired when she was pregnant with twins?" Zee asked Missy.

Missy thought. "I don't really remember," she said. "I was only five when they were born."

"She's not going to be pregnant forever," Ally reassured Zee.

"You're right," Zee said, perking up a little.

Then Zee noticed a strange look on Missy's face. "What?" she asked.

"Well . . ." Missy hesitated.

"What?" Ally pleaded.

"If you think your mom is tired and forgetful now, just

wait till she actually has the babies," Missy explained. Zee's stomach dropped, afraid of what Missy would say next. "Your dad, too. When your parents aren't feeding them, changing their diapers, or giving them baths, they'll be sleeping—probably on the couch."

"Sounds bad," Ally put in.

"It is," Missy said. "You'll forget what homemade snacks taste like."

"I think it would be fun to be a big sister," Chloe said. "The twins will probably think that Zee is the most awesome person in the world."

Zee smiled. Lately, she'd been so busy thinking about losing her parents, she hadn't even considered what she'd be gaining.

"That part's cool," Missy agreed. "Until the screaming starts."

"Screaming?" Zee gulped. "For what?"

"Anything—and *everything*," Missy explained.

"I thought you were too young to remember," Chloe reminded her.

"Oh, I remember the screaming. I recommend you keep your iPod on twenty-four hours a day."

"I'll be here for you, Zee," Ally said. "Just log onto Blue-topia and find me. Oh! That reminds me—" she said to

Jasper. "I know you said we shouldn't invite anyone else, but I was thinking it would be really cool if my French friends were on Bluetopia, too."

"We definitely need more people for the Fashionista group," Missy pointed out.

"Yeah," Chloe agreed. "It would be awesome to get ideas from people I don't already talk to about fashion every day."

Jasper swallowed his mouthful of food and opened his mouth to respond. Zee was certain he was about to say no.

"Ally's right. Bluetopia was supposed to help me and Ally keep in touch without having to always catch up first with what's going on with our friends," Zee reminded Jasper. She looked around the table. "My friends have all joined. Plus, having Ally's friends from Paris would make Bluetopia more international."

Jasper stayed quiet.

"The French definitely like soccer," Chloe added.

That got Jasper's attention. "I suppose we could invite them, too."

"Yay!" the girls cheered.

Jasper pointed his finger. "Only if they promise not to invite anyone else."

Ally made an X over her chest. "Promise!"

Zee couldn't wait to make her next blog entry.

Bloggio,
I'm not sure how to make a chart, and I can't ask anyone since this blog is 100 percent private, so you'll just have to pretend that these lists are in a chart.

Things That Are Going Better Than I Thought
Bluetopia. Everyone loves it, and Jasper is letting more people join, so it's going to be even more fun.

My music career. Who wouldn't want to be Roxy Vardolis's assistant? And two of my songs are going to be featured at the biggest event in Brookdale.

My friendship with Missy. She's full of information about twins.

<u>Things That Are Going Worse Than I Thought</u>

The Soon-to-Be Babies. It sounds like they're not much fun.

Mom. She's definitely changed since she's gotten pregnant.

(I can't think of a third thing, so there are more good things than bad. I hope it lasts.)

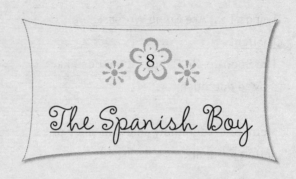

8

The Spanish Boy

Zee was already at breakfast Wednesday morning when Ally came down.

"What took you so long?" Zee asked, digging a section out of her grapefruit with a spoon.

"Sorry." Ally grabbed the container of Mrs. Carmichael's homemade granola from the counter and brought it to the table. "I was on Bluetopia."

"Cool beans!" Zee said. "What's going on?"

"Marcus and Conrad have started a joke blog."

"Is it funny?" Zee asked.

"They're definitely not as funny on the computer screen as they are in person, but a few of the jokes made me laugh."

"What else is going on?"

Ally thought. "Kathi and Jen have created a Dish Club, but it's invitation-only, and since I wasn't invited, I have no idea what that's about."

"I'm sure I won't be invited," Zee said, "so I'll never know, either."

"Oh!" Ally suddenly exclaimed. "I almost forgot about my French friends!"

"Do they like the Fash- ionista Club?" Zee asked.

"No," Ally said with a smile. "They *love* it."

"This is so amazing!" Zee told Ally. "I am going to get to know all of your friends in France the way you got to know my new friends here."

Adam stepped into the kitchen. A lumpy puff of hair stuck out on one side of his head, and his shirt was half- way tucked in.

"Did you wrestle a bear before you came down?" Ally asked.

Zee giggled.

"That's so funny I forgot to laugh," Adam shot back. He opened the refrigerator door. "By the way, don't even think about being my bud."

Zee gagged on her grapefruit juice. "What are you talking about?" she asked after she had recovered.

"Bluetopia." Adam poured himself a glass of milk. "By the way, nice name. Who did you pay to name it after you?"

"How do you know about Bluetopia?" Ally asked, panicked. "You're a senior."

"A bunch of people invited me to be their buds," Adam explained.

"Seventh graders?" Zee asked.

"Uh . . . no. Seniors," Adam responded. "I don't hang out with seventh graders."

"You're here with us," Ally pointed out.

"Exactly. That's already way too much."

"Whatever," Zee said. "How did seniors hear about Bluetopia, anyway?"

Adam shrugged. "I don't know. Word gets around." He chugged his milk and wiped the white mustache from his lip. "I'll give you credit, though. The Beans' page looks awesome. I think you're going to get a bunch of people to come to Brookdale Day to see you."

"That would be so amazing!" Ally squealed. "What if a bunch of talent agents come from L.A. to check us out?"

"Don't get carried away. I just meant that you'll probably get more than the usual seventh graders and their families," Adam told the girls as he walked out of the kitchen. "Bye-o-nara."

"Oh my gosh!" Ally said as Adam disappeared from view. "I think it's my fault there are so many people on Bluetopia."

"Don't freak out," Zee said. "Like Adam said, Bluetopia's going to help The Beans have a larger audience at Brookdale Day."

Ally perked up. "You're right," she said. "It might be the best thing to happen to The Beans."

"But just to be safe," Zee said, "don't invite anyone else."

Chloe met Zee and Ally at the lockers before first period. She looked like she was going to explode. "Guess what?"

"What?" Ally and Zee said at once.

"A Spanish boy likes me!"

"Someone in your Spanish class?" Zee asked.

"No, a boy from Spain," Chloe explained.

"How do you know a Spanish boy?" Zee asked.

"He's on Bluetopia," Chloe said.

"Who invited him to join?" Ally wondered out loud.

Chloe shrugged. "I dunno. But whoever it was, I'm glad they did."

"I don't think it's a good idea to be buds with someone you don't know, Chloe," Zee told her. "It might not be safe."

"I'm not telling him any of my personal information," Chloe explained. "He doesn't even know what town I live in."

"He didn't ask?" Zee said.

"I think you should ask him to tell you who his buds are on the site, Chloe," Ally suggested. "It's kind of weird for him to come out of nowhere."

"Don't worry," Chloe reassured her friends. "I'm not going to do anything stupid. My parents check my Bluetopia page and my email, anyway."

Nearby, laughter interrupted the girls. Zee looked up to see Marcus, Conrad, and Landon walking down the hall.

Ally nudged Zee and whispered, "Here comes Landon."

Zee's stomach only did a tiny somersault. She was surprised that she actually felt close to normal. "Uh . . . yeah," Zee said.

"Don't you like him anymore?" Chloe asked.

"I guess so," Zee told her friends.

As Landon got closer, Zee wondered how she really did

feel. She wasn't getting the flip-flops in her stomach the way she used to. *That's weird!* she thought.

"Hi, Zee," Landon said when he reached her locker.

"Hi," Zee replied. *Think of something to say. Anything,* Zee silently pleaded with herself. "Oh yeah!" she suddenly blurted out. "That was really cool that you posted all of those surfer terms on your Bluetopia page."

"Thanks," Landon said. "It's kind of like a foreign language."

"Cool beans!" Zee said.

"Yeah," Landon agreed.

Then there was an uncomfortable silence while Zee tried to think of something else to say.

"Oh-kay," Marcus broke in. "I hate to interrupt this interesting conversation, but I have something to ask Chloe."

"You do?" Chloe said, biting her lip nervously.

"I was just wondering if you'd seen anything unusual on Bluetopia."

"Like an interesting friend or something," Conrad added.

"That's so weird," Chloe pointed out. "I do have a new friend—in Spain."

"What's her name?" Marcus asked.

"*His* name is José," Chloe corrected him.

"*Ohh,*" Marcus said in a singsong voice. "Is he your *boy*friend?"

Chloe blushed and rolled her eyes. "No, he's just a friend—I mean, bud." Zee could tell Chloe was happy to have something to talk to Marcus about—even if it was another boy.

"How old is he?" Conrad asked.

"Thirteen."

"Does he speak English?"

"Almost as well as I do," Chloe said.

"Almost?" Conrad asked. "What's wrong with his English?"

"Nothing. It's just obvious that it's not his first language."

"Hey, look!" Ally cut in, staring down the hall. "Here comes Jasper."

Now Zee's stomach began flipping and flopping. Was she nervous because she didn't know how Jasper would react to so many new people joining Bluetopia—or was there some other reason?

As Jasper walked toward the group, Zee could see that his white shirt was untucked on one side, and his tie was off-center.

"What happened to you?" Chloe asked.

"You look like you got in a fight on the way to school," Ally said.

"You look like Adam," Zee added.

Jasper looked down at himself, then fixed his shirt and tie. "I was up all night fixing Bluetopia."

"What's wrong with it?" Zee asked.

"Just a lot of traffic."

"Traffic?" Chloe said, confused.

"A lot of people," Jasper explained. "I can't even keep track of everyone. There are kids from so many countries."

"Like Spain?" Marcus asked.

Jasper looked at Marcus curiously, but all he said was "Undoubtedly."

Then Marcus and Conrad gave each other a high five.

"What are you two so happy about?" Zee asked.

The smile disappeared from Conrad's face. "Just that Bluetopia is turning out to be really cool."

"See, Jasper," Zee said proudly. "It's totally worth all the work." She patted him on the back.

"Yes, it is," Jasper said, flashing her a smile.

That was enough to send the flipping and flopping into overdrive.

At that moment, Mr. P walked out of the main office toward the group. He said hello, then stopped cold when he noticed Jasper.

"Did you get into a fight?" Mr. P asked.

"That's what I said," Ally said as the others laughed.

"No, I overslept this morning because I was up late working on Bluetopia," Jasper said.

Mr. P got a curious look. "What's that?"

Jasper sighed. "It's a social networking site I created for fun."

"It doesn't look like you are having fun."

"Jasper has been working super-hard on it, so it's awesome," Zee explained. "I'll show you." She pulled her iPhone out of her locker and logged onto Bluetopia.

The teacher nodded approvingly. "Very impressive, Jasper."

"Show him The Beans' page, Zee," Chloe suggested.

"Cool! This will help us get a lot of attention. How many people are registered?" Mr. P asked Jasper.

"More than a thousand," Jasper told him.

"More than a thousand?" Zee, Chloe, and Ally asked at once.

"That's incredible," Mr. P said. "I just hope you're working as hard on your music and your schoolwork as you are on the site."

Jasper looked at his feet. "Uh, yes, sir."

Mr. P glanced at the clock in the hall. "I've got to get going. You guys should go to the auditorium for class today. Ms. Vardolis wants you to rehearse on a stage." With a wave, he rounded the corner.

"*Are* you working as hard on your schoolwork and music as you are on Bluetopia?" Zee asked Jasper once Mr. P was out of sight.

"Yes . . ." Jasper hesitated. "From this moment on."

As the group headed to the auditorium, Zee was relieved that Landon was too busy laughing with Conrad and Marcus to notice her. Then as they entered the room, she breathed a sigh of relief when Landon walked to the far side of the seats. It's not that she wanted to avoid him, exactly, but it always seemed so hard to think of something to say when he was around.

Kathi and Jen were sitting close together, whispering. They looked up, and Zee could feel the heat of Kathi's eyes burn her.

"Look for a Bluetopia doodle in the Dish Club after rehearsal," Kathi told Jen.

"Is that some kind of code?" Ms. Vardolis asked.

"No," Jen explained. "Bluetopia is a website that Jasper created. A doodle is like a posting. And the Dish is just a section where you can talk about anything."

Ms. Vardolis nodded. "Wow, Jasper! You're not only a talented musician but also a technical wizard."

Jasper blushed and looked down. "Not exactly."

Kathi quickly changed the subject. "Roxy," she began, rushing toward her cousin. "I'd love for you to look at my song. I really trust your judgment."

Ms. Vardolis looked at the sheet music. "This is really inspired," she began. "I can see that you put a great deal of work into it."

"Yay!" Kathi gave a little cheer. "So you want The Beans to perform it?"

Ms. Vardolis frowned a little. "Unfortunately, I'm really tied up right now working out the details for Saturday's show. I don't have time to arrange it for the group."

"I could arrange it," Kathi said enthusiastically.

The assistant teacher shook her head. "Have you ever arranged music before?"

Kathi shifted uncomfortably. "No," she said quietly.

"Maybe another time."

By now, everyone had stopped talking and was staring right at Kathi, who wasn't used to being told no. Kathi's lips twitched, and Zee realized that Kathi wasn't angry. She was embarrassed—and trying not to cry.

"Everyone, get your instruments out and find your place on the stage," Ms. Vardolis instructed, not noticing her cousin's reaction. "We'll start off with the song we worked on yesterday, then rehearse a new one." She waved a piece of paper above her head. "The other song written by Mackenzie."

Kathi rolled her eyes and picked up her violin.

Once everyone was ready to play, Ms. Vardolis suggested, "Why don't you count off, Mackenzie?"

Zee looked at the other musicians. "One, two, three, four!" she shouted, then began strumming her guitar. "If you've got a problem . . . solve it," she sang. "You don't have a reason . . . to quit."

Zee's heart swelled as she listened to The Beans play behind her. Everyone hit the right notes, and Ms. Vardolis had arranged it so that Landon's drums sounded like a beating heart.

Even Kathi seemed to be making her best effort on the violin, soaring up the strings with Missy, who also played violin, at just the right parts.

And when Chloe and Jen sang backup behind Zee, they harmonized so well they sounded like one person.

"Incredible!" Ms. Vardolis applauded when the song was over. "You guys are definitely ready to perform that one. Nice work, everyone, especially the backup singers."

"Yes!" Jen cheered.

"Whatev," Kathi mumbled.

"It's better to sing backup than nothing at all," Jen pointed out cheerfully.

"You're happy to be just the backup. That's the difference between you and me," Kathi moped.

Jen's smile melted into a frown. "One of them," she responded. She turned to Marcus. "That chord progression in the middle was awesome!"

Kathi's jaw dropped open. Zee was just as shocked. Jen rarely challenged Kathi.

"If you guys play Mackenzie's other song as well as you did that one, I wouldn't be surprised if a big label tried to buy it," Ms. Vardolis interrupted the girls.

Landon gave Zee a thumbs-up from behind his drum kit, and Zee could feel . . . nothing. Nothing special for Landon, at least. Although she was excited that The Beans had done such a great job with her song.

Ms. Vardolis handed each student the next song. "Mackenzie, since you are my assistant and the songwriter," she began, "why don't you start us off again?"

Zee swelled with pride. Ms Vardolis was really giving her a chance to lead. And she was going to show her teacher that she could do it. "We'll try it a little slow at first, then work up to the regular tempo," Zee told the band.

As the group played, Ms. Vardolis weaved her way

across the stage, offering suggestions to the musicians and making adjustments to her arrangement.

"Try playing this part a little softer, then build up to the chorus," the teacher told Ally.

Ally smiled. "Okay. Thanks."

Ms. Vardolis leaned over to Chloe, who was playing her cello. "Add a little vibrato here to make the sound fuller," she said, pointing to the page.

Chloe nodded and started wiggling her fingers on the strings.

Then Ms. Vardolis moved over to Kathi and laid her hand on her right shoulder. "If you loosen your grip on the neck of the violin, it will be easier to hit some of these high notes."

Kathi didn't say anything to her cousin, but after that, Zee noticed that she was having an easier time playing the high notes in tune.

"Bravo!" Ms. Vardolis applauded when they came to the end. "With just a little more practice, you should be ready to perform this song, too."

"Should we play it again now?" Zee asked.

Ms. Vardolis nodded. "I just want to make one change." Kathi smirked, pleased that Zee's song wasn't perfect. "I'd like Landon to sing with you on the third verse, Zee. The words are so romantic, it needs a male voice, too." She pointed to a spot on the floor next to Zee. "Please stand here, Landon."

Zee's heart decided to play a drum solo as Landon came to stand next to her. Was the old feeling coming back? How was she going to sing when she could barely swallow?

"Landon, I want you to join in on the part that goes, 'It's love. It's love. That's how I'm feeling. It's great. It's great. My heart is reeling.' Okay?"

Behind her, Zee heard a loud crash. Jasper's music stand had fallen to the floor.

"So sorry," Jasper said, bending down to collect the scattered papers. "I must have knocked it with my bow."

Jasper wasn't the only one out of sorts. Just the thought of singing those words with Landon made Zee's head spin—until they started singing. The song was definitely romantic, but Landon sang like a robot. And Zee wasn't much better. She expected to be nervous about the duet, but she wasn't. And no matter how hard she tried, she couldn't turn the words into feelings.

To make matters worse, Jasper kept losing his place—and hitting the wrong notes.

Ms. Vardolis threw her arms in the air. "Wow!" she said when they finished. She wore a concerned expression.

"Did you like it?" Conrad asked.

"I don't think that's what she's saying," Missy told him.

"You'll need to practice that one extra-hard on your own, or it will definitely not be ready by Saturday," Ms. Vardolis explained.

"I have an idea!" Kathi blurted out. "Everyone can come to my house tonight to practice. We can order pizza for dinner."

Ms. Vardolis smiled for the first time since they'd started the song. "What a great idea, Kathi. I'm sure knowing how you're helping out would make your parents very proud."

Kathi turned to Zee and smirked.

Zee ignored her. She couldn't worry about Kathi at that moment. She grabbed her guitar and walked offstage before Landon could say anything to her about the romantic duet. A jumble of thoughts bounced around in her head. Instead of being excited about singing with Landon, she wasn't sure she wanted to at all. Before Ms. Vardolis suggested their duet, The Beans sounded fantastic. But now the song was closer to being a disaster.

9
Baby Proof.

"I can't wait to see how you fixed Bluetopia last night," Zee told Jasper as they entered the Carmichaels' house that afternoon. Ally was with them.

"First, we eat, then we go on Bluetopia," Jasper insisted.

Ally giggled. "I guess you need your energy to type," she said.

"No problemo." Zee zoomed across the foyer and into the kitchen, expecting to see her mother and a platter of snacks.

Instead, her mother was leaning over the open cabinet door under the sink. A tall man with gray hair stood next to her.

"Uh . . . hi," Zee said to her mother, but she was looking at the stranger.

Mrs. Carmichael said hello to Zee and her friends. "This is Mr. Sterling," she continued. "He's helping me baby-proof the house."

Jasper looked confused. "You want to keep the babies out of the house?" he asked.

Mrs. Carmichael laughed. "To keep them safe," she explained. "I had no idea that our home was so full of dangers."

"But you've already had two babies," Zee reminded her. "What did you do about us?"

Zee's mom laid a hand on her shoulder. "Don't worry. I looked out for you," she assured her. "But now I'll have two babies *at once*. I'll need to be doubly safe."

Zee didn't even bother to ask about snacks this time. She reached into the cabinet and pulled out a pack of popcorn and put it in the microwave. "We have to be at Kathi's house at four o'clock," Zee reminded her mother as she pushed the buttons.

A rush of panic rose in Mrs. Carmichael's face. "Oh no!" she said.

"I texted you at lunch, and you said you would drive us," Zee reminded her. "Did you forget?"

"I'm afraid so, and Mr. Sterling is not even halfway done here."

"But we can't miss the rehearsal!" Zee told her.

"That's okay, Mrs. Carmichael," Jasper told her, taking his cell phone out of his pocket. "My mother can take us."

"Thank you, Jasper. Please tell her I'll pick everyone up."

Really? Zee thought.

"I promise," Mrs. Carmichael said, reading Zee's mind.

Beep. Beep. Beep. The microwave signaled that the popcorn was ready.

Zee poured the snack into a giant bowl, then lifted it off

the counter with two hands. "We're going up to my room until Mrs. Chapman gets us."

As Zee moved up the steps to the second floor, she turned to her friends. "I'm going to change my clothes," she said, passing the bowl off to Ally. She pulled her arms out of her navy blue cardigan. "I picked out the coolest skirt and leggings for the rehearsal this afternoon."

"I'm checking out my Bluetopia page. I sent a ton of people bunnies this morning," Ally explained. "I hope I get some back."

"I'll send you one," Zee said, dashing up the steps in front of her friends. She grabbed her change of clothes from her dresser drawers, then went into her bathroom to put on her new outfit.

When Zee came out, she held a different bead earring up to each earlobe. "Which looks better—the glass beads or the wooden ones?" she asked.

"Wooden," Ally said.

Zee slipped the earrings in, grabbed her laptop off of her desk, and then sat down on her bed. Ally dropped beside her. Jasper began typing on his own computer that he pulled out of his backpack.

"Can I go first?" Zee said.

"Sure," Ally agreed. "If I can watch."

With Ally beside her, Zee wouldn't be able to write a blog entry, but she could still do a lot on Bluetopia.

"Oh my gosh!" Zee said as her first notice popped up. A bunny wearing a smiley-face T-shirt danced in a box on the screen. "Missy sent me a Smile Bunny. It's so cute."

"Send her a bunny back," Ally suggested.

"I'm going to give her the exact same one."

"Why?" Ally asked.

"It will be like we're twins," Zee told her. "Get it?"

"Awesome!" Ally said.

After Zee sent the bunny to Missy, she checked out her buds' updates.

"Look what Jen wrote," Ally said to Zee. "'Jen Calverez needs a ride to tonight's rehearsal with The Beans. Come see us play at Brookdale Day on Saturday!' We should all advertise the show in our page updates and notebook doodles."

"Jasper!" Zee called to him. "Did you hear what Ally said?"

Jasper's fingers clacked the keyboard. "Yes, it's a brilliant idea," he said without taking his eyes off of the computer screen. "I'll have to do it later, though. I'm still making a few adjustments to the site's programming." He typed some more.

"Oh, and post a doodle telling Jen my mum can take her since she lives near us," Jasper continued. "I'll text Mum and let her know." He kept one hand on the computer while he texted on his cell phone with his other hand.

Ding! Zee's laptop announced that someone wanted to chat with her.

"Oh, look!" Ally said. "It's from Landon."

Landon says: Hi appeared in a box on the screen.

Zee looked over at Jasper and noticed that he stopped typing. But he didn't turn around. "Uh . . . yeah," she said.

"What are you going to say?" Ally asked.

Zee shrugged. "I guess I'll say hi back," Zee said as she typed.

Landon says: Do u want a ride 2 Kathi's?

"That's awesome!" Ally exclaimed when she saw the question.

"I already have a ride," Zee said. "With Jasper's mom."

"Jasper!" Ally called to him.

Jasper finally turned around. "What?"

"Do you care if Zee gets a ride with Landon to Kathi's?" Ally asked. "I'll still go with you."

"That's—"

"I'm not going with Landon," Zee interrupted Jasper.

"You don't want to go with Landon?" Ally asked.

"It's not that," Zee defended herself.

"So what is it?"

"I'd just rather ride with you guys," Zee explained.

"We're going to leave soon," Ally reminded Zee. "Can I log onto Bluetopia now?"

Zee signed off and slid the computer to Ally. "It's all yours."

Ally entered her screen name and password.

"Ohmylanta!" Zee said. Ally had a long list of notices telling her that people had posted in her notebook, sent her gifts, and labeled her in photos. "You're popular!"

"Oh, most of these are from Missy," Ally pointed out. "I think she sent me ten bunnies."

"Really?" Zee leaned in to get a closer look. Ally was right. Missy had sent Ally lots of bunnies, a couple of private messages, three notebook doodles, and one group invitation.

Zee felt a tug of jealousy. She had thought that she and Missy were getting to be better friends because of the twins, but now she realized Missy was much closer to Ally. It was weird to see the proof right on the screen.

"Hey, Zee, look!" Ally said. "The Fashionista Club has seventy-three members."

"Cool beans!" Zee exclaimed. "More of your French friends signed up."

Jasper suddenly pivoted in his chair and wiped his fore-head with his palm. "Seventy-three members? For a fashion club?"

"I know. Isn't it cool?" Ally said.

"Everyone loves Bluetopia," Zee cheered.

"Most of the ideas were yours," Jasper reminded her. "I just did the programming. Now, unfortunately, I'm still doing the programming to make sure it doesn't crash. I had no idea that Bluetopia would take up so much time. I've hardly been able to think about anything else."

"What else is there?" Ally joked.

"Brookdale Day, for one," Jasper said. "If I mess that up, it could hurt my music grade." He looked at the computer screen. "But if Bluetopia crashes, it could be an international disaster."

"You worry way too much," Zee told him. "It's not going to crash. It's perfect." Then she turned to Ally. "We should upload those pictures of the stuff we got at the thrift shop the other day."

"Everyone can suggest how we should mix and match all the different clothes," Ally added.

"Then we can vote," Zee agreed.

Jasper's phone buzzed with a text. "My mum is here to pick us up," he told the girls.

"Rehearsal time!" Zee announced, grabbing her guitar.

Ally logged off, and the three of them hurried downstairs.

Zee found her mother and Mr. Sterling at the bottom of the steps. Mrs. Carmichael wore a serious expression as Mr. Sterling explained, "You'll need a gate that locks."

"We're going to Kathi's now," Zee told her mom.

"All right, honey," Mrs. Carmichael said without looking at her.

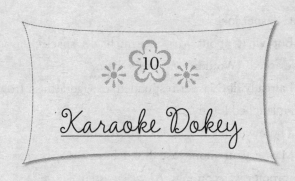

10

Karaoke Dokey

$\mathcal{M}$rs. Chapman had already picked up Chloe from soccer practice on the way to rehearsal. Jen was sitting next to her in the minivan.

"You'll never guess what my mom was doing when I got home this afternoon," Zee blurted out as she fastened her seat belt.

"Taking a nap?" Chloe asked.

"Not this time," Zee told her. "She was talking to someone about baby-proofing the house."

Chloe raised an eyebrow. "What does that mean?"

"It means I'm probably going to have to know a secret code to open a cabinet, go up steps, or lift the toilet lid."

"Perhaps we should start hanging out at my house

more," Jasper joked.

"But what about Mrs. Carmichael's snacks, Jasper?" Chloe asked. "Wouldn't you miss them?"

"I already do," Jasper responded, exaggerating a frown.

Jen laughed loudly.

"There weren't any," Zee said. "Again."

"Maybe your mom just didn't have time, because the baby-proofer was coming," Ally suggested.

"I bet it just slipped her mind," Mrs. Chapman called from the driver's seat in her British accent. "I remember when I was pregnant with Jaspy."

"Jaspy?" Zee silently mouthed.

Jasper buried his hands in his face.

"What happened?" Chloe asked.

"I forgot everything," Mrs. Chapman began. "I would pick up the phone and forget who I was calling. I'd drive to the grocery store and end up at the bank."

"Is that normal?" Ally asked.

"It doesn't happen to every woman, but a lot of people do have trouble remembering things when they get pregnant."

"When my mom was pregnant with my little sister, she wore slippers to work once," Jen told them.

The seventh graders laughed.

"See, Zee? It's perfectly normal," Chloe said.

"I guess," Zee agreed. "I can't worry about it now, anyway. I need to focus on the performance on Saturday."

"We all do," Chloe said, looking at the others. "Right?"

"Now that Bluetopia is running smoothly, I will be able to practice as much as it takes to make The Beans the stars of Brookdale Day," Jasper said.

Zee turned to Jen. "That was a really good idea to mention Brookdale Day in your update," she said. "We're all going to do that."

"Thanks!" Jen said. "I love Bluetopia. I'm making so many new friends."

"Oh, that reminds me, José sent me a bunch of doodles right before I got home from school." Chloe blushed. "He says he likes my green eyes."

"How does he know you have green eyes?" Zee asked.

"I have a bunch of photos on my Bluetopia page."

"So what does he look like?" Ally said.

"Like a model," Chloe said.

"Really?" Zee asked.

"Yeah. He only has one picture, but I swear it belongs in a magazine. He's so gorgeous."

"Wow, Chloe!" Jen exclaimed as the minivan stopped in front of Kathi's house. "That's so awesome."

Zee looked from one friend to the next. It was great to see Chloe so happy, but was she the only one with a funny feeling about mysterious José?

As Zee and her friends approached the Barneys' house, the front door flew open. Mrs. Barney stood inside it with a huge smile across her face. "Welcome, everyone! Please come inside. It's so nice to have you here. I was so pleased Roxy— I mean, Ms. Vardolis—told us that Kathi had stepped up and shown her strong leadership skills. I think that's what a group like this needs."

Ally stared at Kathi's mother with wide eyes. "Uh-huh."

"Of course, she gets it from my side of the family. I'm sure you can see that in Ms. Vardolis—and me."

Chloe nodded. "Totally," she said unenthusiastically.

Zee looked around. "Um . . . where is Kathi?"

Mrs. Barney placed her hand on her chest and gave a phony chuckle. "Oh my! I almost forgot." She pointed toward the back of the house. "She's all set up on the patio."

"By the pool?" Zee asked.

"Yes! I know that most of your families don't have swimming pools as big as mine, so I thought this would be fun."

Zee began walking toward the back of the house. "Definitely," she said. The others followed.

Kathi clapped when she saw the others. "Yay! Everyone's here now."

But Zee could barely hear because she was so distracted by the scene before her. The patio had been transformed into a Hawaiian luau. Tiki torches surrounded the pool. Landon was piling his plate with food from a table full of colorful platters. Missy wore a real flower lei around her neck. Conrad and Marcus were sitting on lounge chairs, sipping drinks in hollow pineapple shells through straws.

"Wow!" Jasper exclaimed.

"I thought we were having pizza," Chloe said.

"Oh, I just said that," Kathi said. "My mom would never serve guests pizza. As soon as I told her everyone was coming over, she called our caterers."

"You really didn't need to go to so much trouble," Zee pointed out.

"Yes, I did!" Kathi said, then corrected herself. "The Beans deserve to be treated well, and the Barneys know how to do that."

Ally snorted. Then everyone stared at her. "Oh, sorry,"

she apologized. "I must be getting a cold."

"Anyway," Kathi said dismissively. She turned to the others and raised her voice. "Let's warm up with some karaoke."

"I thought we were going to practice for Brookdale Day," Zee said.

"We are," Kathi said firmly. "But we're going to have a little fun first."

"Yeah!" Conrad said to Zee. "Let's have some fun first."

Marcus got out of his chair and grabbed the microphone. "I'll go first!"

Missy sat down in front of Marcus. "Ally, sit next to me," she said.

Ally headed across the patio, and Zee followed. The others found a spot around them.

Marcus started pushing some buttons on the karaoke machine. "What are you going to sing, Marcus?" Landon asked.

"You'll find out when I start singing," Marcus told him. Then he put the mike up to his mouth and nodded to Kathi.

"'If I were a boy, even just for a day,'" he quietly crooned along to the music.

"Oh no!" Conrad shouted as the others cracked up. Marcus was singing a Beyoncé song.

Marcus kept singing above the laughter, belting out the chorus as loudly as he could and nodding his head furiously each time he got to the part in the chorus, "I think I'd be a better man."

Conrad leaped onstage after him to perform Rihanna's "Take a Bow." Each time he sang "How 'bout a round of applause," he motioned for everyone to clap. When he finished, he yelled, "A standing ovation!" The seventh graders stood and cheered.

Then Kathi did a serious interpretation of Miley Cyrus's "The Climb," and Jen wowed the crowd with Whitney Houston's classic "Where Do Broken Hearts Go?"

After that, Missy bounded toward the stage as Ally started to get up. "Ally and I are going to sing a duet."

"Really?" Zee asked.

"Uh . . . yeah," Ally said. "That's okay, right?"

"Definitely," Zee said, although it sounded more like, "No."

Chloe leaned closer to Zee. "I know the perfect song for us to sing together," she whispered.

Zee smiled. *Good old Chloe!* Knowing Chloe was there for Zee made it easier to watch Ally and Missy having so much fun—without her.

When Ally and Missy finished singing their duet from *High School Musical*, Chloe grabbed Zee's arm. "Our turn!" Chloe announced.

"What are we singing?" Zee asked.

"It's a surprise," Chloe explained.

"From me?" Zee said. "How can I sing if I don't know what I'm singing?"

Chloe shook her head. "Don't worry. As soon as the music comes up, you'll know just what to do."

Chloe made her selection and the music began to play. As soon as it did, Zee really did know what to do. It was a song from *Toy Story*.

"'You've got a friend in me,'" Chloe sang. Zee loved the fact that it was totally corny—and true.

"'You've got a friend in me,'" Zee sang back.

They sang the song together, switching off parts, joining arms, and kicking their legs in sync to the beat. But the
best part was that Zee knew Chloe meant every word of
the lyrics.

"I never realized what a great song that was," Zee said
when the music faded out.

"Awesome, huh?" Chloe hurried back to her spot in the
audience.

"Who wants to go next?" Zee asked, holding out the
microphone.

"Landon!" Conrad volunteered his friend.

Landon shook his head. "No way am I doing karaoke."

"Are you too cool, surfer dude?" Marcus joked.

"Pretty much," Landon said.

"Jasper?" Zee said, but as all eyes turned in his direction, she immediately regretted saying anything. Jasper hated to be the focus of attention. She hadn't meant to embarrass him.

"Okay," Jasper agreed, standing.

"Really?" Landon asked.

"Really?" Zee echoed.

Jasper took the microphone from Zee. "No reason to be a stick-in-the-mud." He looked at Landon.

"Do they say that in England a lot?" Landon asked. "Because I don't even know what it means."

"It means this." Jasper started the music. "'One for the money! Two for the show!'" He pretended to play a fake guitar just like Elvis Presley. He slid across the patio and spun around.

"Whoa!" Landon whispered to himself.

Zee couldn't believe her eyes, either! Was this shy Jasper? Her heart tried to jump out of her chest. She'd never seen him perform with so much spirit—having so much fun as he wiggled his hips and tapped his toes in time to the music. Zee wondered if he could see her blushing.

"Let's go again," Kathi suggested when Jasper finished.

Zee checked the time on her iPhone. "I think we should practice our music for Saturday."

"Oh, come on," Kathi urged. "You're spoiling everyone's fun."

"My mom's coming to get me soon," Zee explained.

"And I have a ton of homework to do," Jen said, pulling out her marimba mallets.

Kathi stared at Jen. She looked like she didn't know what to say. Then when the other group members started to get their instruments ready, she just said, "Fine," and took out her violin.

Kathi had been so proud of how she'd pulled the group together, Zee hated to spoil her moment. But The Beans needed to practice. With so many people hearing about their upcoming performance on Bluetopia, they had to be ready.

"Let's practice 'My Heart,'" Kathi suggested when everyone was in position. "It needs the most work, especially Zee's part."

Zee rolled her eyes, but as the band began to play, she could tell everyone had taken Ms. Vardolis's advice seriously. The band members hit their parts perfectly. And something inside Zee changed as she sang along with Landon. She kept picturing Jasper on the karaoke stage. The words flowed out of her mouth without her even thinking.

"Your idea for us to warm up with karaoke helped," Missy told Kathi. "We sounded great."

"Roxy is going to be really proud when she hears us tomorrow," Kathi said.

⁕ 11 ⁕

Bad Buds

fter rehearsal, Zee, Ally, Chloe, and Jasper waited for Mrs. Carmichael outside of the Barneys' house. Zee pulled out her iPhone and looked at its clock.

"That's about the hundredth time you've checked," Ally told her. "I think your mom forgot again."

"But she said she'd come, and she's not picking up the house phone," Zee pointed out. "She must be on her way."

"Try her cell phone again," Chloe suggested. "Maybe she turned it back on."

"Perhaps we should call my mom to pick us up," Jasper

said, looking around. "It's getting late, and everyone else has left." Even Jen's mom had come to get her after work.

Zee couldn't stand the thought that her mother might have forgotten about her again. She was determined to wait until Mrs. Carmichael showed up. But how long would that take? It had already been thirty minutes.

Zee's iPhone buzzed in her hand. "A text from Mom," she announced triumphantly, pleased her mother had not forgotten her after all.

Where r u? the text read. I've been waiting outside BA a long time.

"BA," Zee read out loud, then told her friends. "My mom is looking for us at school." She was picking them up at the wrong place!

Zee quickly texted her mother back to tell her to come to Kathi's house.

Then Chloe took out her cell phone.

"What are you doing?" Zee asked.

"Going on Bluetopia, of course," Chloe said. "To see if José made any doodles in my notebook or sent me any gifts."

"I guess you don't like Marcus anymore," Ally teased.

"Of course I do," Chloe protested. "He's just not writing me as much as José is." She looked at her screen. "I got something!"

"I think José needs to sleep," Zee said. "It's like"—she paused to calculate the time difference between California and Spain—"three A.M. there."

"There's your mom!" Ally shouted, pointing to Mrs. Carmichael's Prius as it came down the block. "I call shotgun!"

"I guess I'll take the hump in the back since I'm the smallest," Zee volunteered. But as she crawled into the car after Jasper and settled into the small space between him and Chloe, she realized she'd forgotten how squished she'd be—right next to Jasper. As a warm, happy feeling rushed through her body, she realized she didn't really care. She waited until she got home to write on her blog.

Hi, Blogness,

Problem #1: I'm trying to be really positive about the idea of having new sibs. Babies are *incredibly* cute. I guess that's why it's a problem. Being adorable will get them a lot of attention. Maybe all of it.

　　Solution #1: The Beans' performance is taking my mind off my mom and babies. Plus, Ms. Vardolis is giving me all of the attention my mother isn't. She's not exactly my mother, but I

---

really like her and am flattered that she thinks I'm so talented. So until Mom can start paying attention to me again, I think I'll just focus on all the nice things Ms. Vardolis says about me. ☺

Problem #2: I don't get what is going on with Ms. Vardolis and Kathi. Something doesn't feel exactly right. Kathi is trying so hard to impress her—too hard. And I think Kathi is blaming me when things go wrong.

Solution #2: Watch out for Kathi! She might take her anger out on me.

Problem #3: I'm 99.99999 percent certain I have a crush on Jasper. Here are the signs:

• my heart beats fast when he's around

• my palms get sweaty (which is really gross) when he's around

• everything he says sounds super-smart

• my head gets all mushy when I think about him

• I think the school uniform actually looks good on him

I don't get it. Why do I like him so much now? He's one of my very best friends. Am I going to ruin that because of a crush??!!

> Solution #3: Forget about Jasper being my boyfriend. Right?
>
> Zee

After Zee finished her blog entry, she visited the Fashionista Club. She wanted to see what people said about the photos she had posted. But she definitely wasn't ready for what she read.

Next to a photo of Zee in a flowing cotton skirt and a denim midriff top with a camisole underneath, someone had posted: When was this ever in fashion?

Under a picture of Zee's favorite homemade sundress, a red tank top sewn onto a floral skirt, was the message: Time to milk the cows!

Scrolling down the page, Zee saw that all of the messages were similar. At first, Zee thought she had finally found a compliment. Very American! Then she kept reading. Leave fashion to the French.

Zee's heart sank to the bottom of her shoes. Ally's French friends were posting these mean comments. Zee knew her style wasn't like everyone else's, but that's what she liked best about it. It wasn't French—or American. It was Zee.

But Zee had an even bigger problem than fashion. How

was Zee going to tell her BFF that some of her new friends weren't very nice?

"Look at what people are saying in the Fashionista Club notebook," Zee said as calmly as she could.

Ally looked at the computer screen, then shrugged. "They aren't being mean. They just think about fashion in a different way."

The comment stung. Ally was supposed to be her very best friend. How could she stick up for them? *I'm the one she should be defending*, Zee thought.

"But—" Zee stopped herself. Ally would be in town for only a few days, and Zee didn't want to fight with her. It wasn't Ally Zee was mad at. It was those French girls.

Still, the comments hurt, so when Ally went to play Wii, Zee sent a private message to Chloe and Jasper.

C&J,
Check out the Fashionista Club and you'll see how horrible Ally's French friends are. She must be so happy to be in Brookdale with us, because they are really really mean. I'm lucky to have you guys. So is Ally.
Zee

Almost immediately, Jasper sent a message back.

Do you want me to take the comments down? The administrator can do that.—J

How sweet! Zee thought, smiling. *Jasper would do that for me?* Then she typed a response.

No, if it doesn't bother Ally, it's OK with me.

Secretly, though, Zee hoped that Ally would ask the French girls to take down the comments.

Ally's friends weren't the only things bothering Zee at that moment. She kept thinking about how her mother had forgotten her that afternoon. Chloe, Ally, and Jasper told her everything was going to be okay. But based on the way Mrs. Carmichael had been acting, Zee found it hard to believe. Zee realized there was only one person who would know for sure . . . Missy.

Missy,
OMG! My mother is completely losing it!! She left me stranded after rehearsal today! Can u believe it??!! I don't think I'm ready 2 have twins. ☹
Please send me some good advice.
Zee

12

Games

When Zee woke up on Thursday, her heart pounded as though she'd just sprinted around the block. Then a moment from her dream flashed through her mind. Zee opened her laptop and began typing.

Hello, Blog,

OMG! I just had a dream about Jasper! It was ~~really strange~~ totally bizarro. We held hands!!! And I liked it. It wasn't weird at all. I mean, in my dream it wasn't weird. In real life, it would be really weird. Right?

I have to find out. I have to see if I like Jasper *like that* for real.

Sleepy Zee

More than ever, Zee wanted to get to the bottom of how she felt about Jasper. But how? Zee knew the answer—she had to see Jasper. School started in an hour. She'd see him in first period as usual.

Unless, Zee thought, *I can come up with a reason to see him before*.

As Zee's eyes fell on her computer, the excuse was obvious. That was it! Bluetopia! She'd had an idea for Jasper to add some games to the site so buds could play one another. This was the perfect time to talk to him about it. Zee texted him.

>Cn my dad pick u up this AM 4 skool? I need 2 talk 2 u.

Jasper's answer came right away.

>Is everything OK?
>Yes. I just have an idea.
>What?

Zee realized that Jasper might not think it was as urgent for them to get together as she did.

>I'll tell u later.

As Zee sent the message, Ally woke up. "What are you doing?" she asked suspiciously.

"What do you mean?"

"You have a look on your face like you're planning something."

"Oh . . . uh . . . no," Zee said. "Not really. I'm just going to have Dad pick up Jasper on the way to school."

"But school is that way," Ally said, pointing in the direction of the Carmichaels' front yard. "And Jasper lives that way," she finished, pointing the opposite direction.

Zee moved across her bedroom to her closet and began searching for her black high-top Converse. She had covered them in black sequins. "Yeah, we'll have to leave a little earlier than usual."

"Is everything all right?" Ally asked.

"Perfect!" Zee assured her. "It's just with all of the practicing for Brookdale Day, I'm not sure when I'll get to talk to him about my latest idea for Bluetopia."

"How about at lunch?" Ally asked.

Zee shook her head and thought fast. "I don't want everyone listening in. What if he doesn't like the idea?"

"What is it, anyway?"

"Uh . . . I think Bluetopia's creator should hear it first," Zee told her.

"Still, I don't understand why you can't just tell him at school," Ally said.

Zee knew she couldn't say, "Because I have to find out if I like Jasper," so she just said, "We have to hurry up and get ready so we can pick up Jasper and get to school on time."

"Well, I'm taking a shower," Ally told her.

"Hurry!"

As Ally shut the bathroom door behind her, Zee sat down at her computer again.

Hi, Blogary,

Ally is my BFF. I always tell her about my crushes. All of them. So why not Jasper? What's the big deal?

Here are my theories:

1. I feel bad about having a crush on Jasper, because I'm worried it could make my other friendships weird. Ally, Chloe, Jasper, and I are a group of four. What will happen if Jasper and I are a couple? Will that break up the group?

2. I'm not really sure if I have a crush on Jasper. Maybe I just want to be certain.

3. If Jasper doesn't like me back, I'd be majorly embarrassed if anyone else knew. Even Ally.

When Zee heard the shower water stop running, she logged off and scrambled to put on her school uniform.

"Your vest is on backward," Ally told Zee as she walked out of the bathroom, her head wrapped up in a towel.

Zee felt as though she had been caught doing something wrong. She pulled her arms back through the holes and twisted the vest around. "I guess I'm just trying to get ready really fast." She grabbed a pair of footless tights with black-and-white cartoon faces out of her top drawer and rushed to pull them on.

"Do you like these?" Zee asked, modeling the tights for Ally.

"Yeah," Ally said. "They're cool."

Zee pulled a pair of knee-high gray and blue socks out of the drawer. "Are these better?"

"What you have on is fine," Ally pointed out.

"I know, but I need my outfit to be more than fine." Zee looked at Ally, who was wearing a jean jacket with cargo pants and a fitted white T-shirt. "I feel like a Fashion Don't in this awful uniform."

"The tights you have on are fabulous. And with your Converse, you'll look great."

Zee smiled. "Thanks."

"Now let's go get some breakfast," Ally said, heading out the bedroom door.

Mr. Carmichael came into the kitchen, poured some coffee into his travel mug, and screwed the top on. "Let's go, girls," he said, looking at his watch. "I've got a meeting this morning."

"Okay, Dad," Zee said, grabbing her bowl, then picking up Ally's, which still had oatmeal in it.

"Hey!" Ally protested. "I'm not finished."

"My dad says we have to go," Zee explained. She loaded the dishes into the dishwasher, then turned around, looking on all the countertops for her lunch. "Where are our lunches?" she asked her mother, who was sitting on a stool at the island reading a book called *What to Expect When You're Expecting.*

Mrs. Carmichael kept reading. "I didn't make you one."

"What?" Zee asked. "Why not?"

Zee's mother looked up and smiled. "Sweetie, you always buy hot lunch on Fridays," she said.

"Mom?" Zee began. "It's Thursday."

"Oh, I'm so sorry," Mrs. Carmichael apologized. "I keep mixing things up. I guess my head hasn't been screwed on straight lately."

"The Carmichael train is leaving the station!" Zee's father announced.

"I'll make you lunch and take you to school this morning," Mrs. Carmichael said.

Zee could tell her mother felt bad and wanted to make up for her mistakes, but Zee had her morning planned already. "No, I promised Jasper we'd pick him up," she explained. "We don't really have time. We'll just buy lunch today."

The girls grabbed their backpacks, kissed Mrs. Carmichael good-bye, and headed toward the garage.

Zee started to climb into the backseat of her father's black SUV.

"You don't want to sit up front with me, Zee?" Mr. Carmichael asked.

Zee figured "I'd rather sit in back with Jasper" probably wasn't the best answer, so she said, "It'll be easier to talk to Jasper if I sit back here."

"I'll ride shotgun, J.P.," Ally said, opening the passenger door. After she fastened her seat belt, she pulled out a hairbrush and began fixing her hair.

Oh, no! Zee had been in such a hurry, she'd forgotten to brush her own red bob. She frantically began to comb it with her fingers.

"Why did Jasper need a ride this morning?" Mr. Carmichael asked Zee as they pulled out of the driveway. "Is everything okay with his parents?"

"Everything is fine," Zee assured him, pulling and twisting the strands that wouldn't cooperate. "I just needed to . . . uh . . . meet with him."

A smile spread across Mr. Carmichael's face. "Like a business meeting?"

"That's it!" Zee said, a little too enthusiastically. "I need to talk to him about Bluetopia."

"Oh yes. Adam said you and your friends had created a really great site," Mr. Carmichael said.

"Adam said it was 'really great'?" Zee asked.

"I believe his exact word was 'awesome'! How's that going?"

"Incredible!" Ally said. "Zee is finally meeting my amazing new French friends. Right, Zee?" She looked back at Zee and smiled.

"Yeah, the site is so cool," Zee said, dodging Ally's question. "Jasper did a really great job."

"Zee had lots of fantastic ideas, too," Ally explained.

"I think it's nice that you and Jasper are working together on it," Mr. Carmichael said. As the SUV pulled into the Chapmans' driveway, Jasper came out of the house.

Zee's heart pounded. "It is."

When Jasper climbed into the car, he greeted everyone. "Hi, guys."

"Hi, Jasper," Zee said.

"Thank you for driving me this morning, Mr. Carmichael," Jasper said.

"Not a problem," Mr. Carmichael told him.

"It kind of was a problem for me," Ally said.

"Hey!" Zee joked, playfully kicking the back of the passenger seat.

"Your text on my mobile seemed rather important," Jasper said.

Zee looked his way. *I can't believe I've never noticed how*

incredibly brown Jasper's eyes are, she thought.

"Zee?" Jasper asked.

"Huh?"

"What did you want to talk to me about?"

Oh my god! How long have I been staring at him? "You should put some games on Bluetopia so that buds can play against one another."

"That's a brilliant idea!" Jasper said. "I'll start working on it during study hall today."

Zee smiled. "Great!"

"That's it?" Ally protested.

"Yes," Zee told her.

"The meeting's over?"

Zee nodded. "Yup."

"I practically had to swallow my breakfast in one gulp. I didn't get a chance to blow-dry my hair. I—"

"If you forgive Zee for rushing you this morning," Jasper interrupted, "I'll forgive you for inviting Missy to join Bluetopia and overloading the site."

"Deal!" Ally agreed quickly. She turned around in her seat and didn't complain about getting up early again.

13

Some Gum

$\mathcal{Z}$ee did a double take as she, Jasper, Chloe, and Ally walked through the main doors of Brookdale Academy on Friday morning. "Hey, look!" She stared straight ahead at a girl with short black hair putting books into a locker. "A new student."

Chloe squinted her eyes. "Isn't that the same teddy bear backpack as Missy's?"

"And that's Missy's locker," Ally pointed out. "That's Missy!" She rushed ahead toward Missy, and the others hurried to catch up. "Oh my gosh! I love your hair so much," Ally told Missy when she got to the locker.

Pools of tears formed in the corners of Missy's eyes. "I don't like it at all."

Thud. Missy closed her locker hard, but because it was made of wheat board it didn't make much noise.

"Why did you get it cut?" Zee asked.

"My brothers put gum in my hair," Missy explained.

Chloe gasped. "On purpose?"

Missy nodded.

"Couldn't you just cut the gum out?" Zee asked.

"It was right at the top of my head," Missy said. "My father tried to cut it out, but my hair looked horrible."

"Ugh!" Ally said. "How long do you think it'll take to grow back?"

"I have no idea," Missy told her. "I've had long hair practically my whole life."

Ally and Missy walked slightly ahead of Zee, Chloe, and Jasper toward their first-period classroom. "I'm glad I don't have little siblings," Ally said.

"You should be," Missy assured her.

A shudder ran up Zee's back as she touched her hair. Would her new

siblings do horrible things to her? With two against one and Adam away at college, she wouldn't stand a chance. Luckily, Zee could forget her worries during first period. "One, two, three, four!" Zee counted off the beat for one of the songs the band would play at Brookdale Day. The Beans followed her lead and started out strong. As she sang, Zee decided to have a little fun. She weaved her way across the stage, leaning in with her guitar to play along with Marcus and Jen. Then she walked over to Missy and Kathi and sang into their microphone.

Next she moved between Landon and Conrad. Landon flashed Zee a big smile. She smiled back, but she noticed that she didn't feel any different than when Conrad took his sax out of his mouth and did the same.

When Chloe and Ally had a short duet, Zee stood beside them in a *ta-da* pose. It all came so naturally. Zee felt like a real rock star.

The most fun came when Zee and Jasper spontaneously broke away from Ms. Vardolis's arrangement. Zee sidled up to Jasper and strummed the melody on the guitar. Jasper looked her in the eyes and thumped out a response on his bass.

And when the song was over, everyone cheered. "I don't see any reason to rehearse that one again," Ms. Vardolis told them. "Play it just like that on Saturday, and it will be perfect."

"Go, Zee!" Ally cheered and the others joined in—except Kathi, who stood with her arms crossed.

Jasper beamed at Zee. Suddenly, the easiness she had felt when she was singing disappeared. She looked at her feet to hide the red rising to her face.

"Ally, are you sure you have to go back to France?" Ms. Vardolis joked. "You're definitely one of The Beans."

Ally smiled and looked down at her casual clothes. "Except for the uniform."

Everyone laughed. Then Ms. Vardolis slapped her hand across her mouth. "We haven't even talked about what to wear tomorrow."

"I think—" Jasper began.

"Don't you dare suggest we wear our school uniforms!" Conrad interrupted him. "You're the only one who likes them."

Everyone laughed—even Jasper. "I was actually thinking we should all wear blue jeans and T-shirts," Jasper continued. "Everyone could pick a different color."

"All right, Jasper!" Ally cheered. "I didn't know you were into fashion. You should join the Fashionista Club."

"I don't think I'm quite ready for that," Jasper said.

"I like it," Ms. Vardolis said. "But let's see what the rest of the band thinks."

Kathi spoke up right away. "I saw some great jackets at a boutique. We could each buy one to wear. They were only like two hundred dollars."

Chloe gasped. "I don't think my parents will buy me a two-hundred-dollar jacket."

"Maybe Brookdale Academy would pay for them," Kathi suggested. She looked hopefully at Ms. Vardolis.

"There are too many other things the music department needs more than jackets," Ms. Vardolis said to Kathi. "Let's hear what the others think of Jasper's idea."

"Sounds good to me," Marcus said. Landon nodded.

"Me too," Conrad put in.

Missy pulled on the ends of her hair. "I'm kind of worried that I'll end up looking just like the boys in a T-shirt and blue jeans."

"I have an idea!" Zee blurted out. "Anybody who wants to can come to my house after school. We can decorate the T-shirts with jewels and sparkles."

"Uh . . . no thanks," Marcus said. "I'm not the sparkly type."

Zee giggled. "Yours can be plain."

"Why don't we put each band member's name on the

back," Chloe suggested. "Like a soccer jersey."

"Brilliant!" Jasper said.

"I think it's a great way to show The Beans' spirit of teamwork," Ms. Vardolis agreed.

Kathi rolled her eyes. "Jen and I already have something to do after school," she said. "Right, Jen?"

Jen gave the others a "sorry" face and nodded.

Ms. Vardolis called to Kathi. "Can you please come see me this afternoon before you leave for the day?" she asked. "I'd like to talk to you about something."

Kathi flicked her head so that her long brown hair moved off her face. "What?" she asked.

"I have a couple of ideas about how you can make your part in the final piece sound a little more rock-and-roll."

Zee was surprised. Kathi hadn't been happy when she found out she couldn't sing lead, but she had been working hard anyway. Zee thought she sounded just as good as Missy.

"I can't, Roxy," Kathi told her. "Mom wants me to come home after school."

"I already talked to Aunt Roni, and she says it's fine for a little while," Ms. Vardolis explained.

"Then I guess I'll see you after school." Kathi closed her violin case.

Mr. P entered the room. "Hello, Beans. I just stopped by to let you know that there's going to be a big surprise for you at Brookdale Day tomorrow," he said.

"I love surprises!" Jen cheered. "What is it?"

"If I told you, it wouldn't be a surprise," Mr. P told her.

"I'm cool with that," Marcus said. "You can tell me."

"You'll have to be cool with not knowing until tomorrow," Mr. P said. "Too late now, anyway," Mr. P added, "the bell is about to ring. First period is just about over."

"I feel like there's a new surprise every day," Zee told Ally and Chloe as they put their instruments away. "First Ally shows up in Brookdale, then my mom is pregnant, then Ms. Vardolis joins our class, and we're performing at Brookdale Day . . . ," she ticked off.

"What do you think the next one's going to be?" Chloe asked, bouncing with excitement.

"I've given up on even trying to figure it out," Zee said. "I just hope it's good."

As the rest of The Beans gathered their books, Ms. Vardolis waved her arms in the air. "I almost forgot, I have an announcement."

"Was Zee crowned Queen of the World?" Kathi half-whispered to Jen.

Jen shrugged.

"I got a call from the Brookdale Day coordinator. She wants to make The Beans the opening act on Brookdale Day," Ms. Vardolis explained. "To start the day off with a bang."

Chloe, Ally, Missy, and Zee jumped and clapped in a circle while Landon gave Marcus and Conrad high fives. Missy and Jen gave each other a hug. Even Kathi wore a smile. And Jasper shook each band member's hand. Before he could grab hers, Zee quickly wiped off her sweaty palm on her pants so he wouldn't know how nervous he had made her. Of course, it just got sweaty again when he shook it.

With the buzz in the room, Zee didn't notice that Landon had come over. "It's kind of interesting to see Jasper onstage," Landon remarked.

"What do you mean?" Zee asked.

Landon half-shrugged. "He's kind of like a different person. Don't you think? Like he's two-faced."

Zee glanced over at Jasper, who was quietly putting his bass into its case. *Or maybe we've just never noticed the* real *Jasper before*, she thought. But out loud, she said, "I don't think that's it." Zee zipped her guitar case. "I've gotta go," she told Landon. "I don't want to be late for second period."

Ms. Vardolis gave Zee some costume money, so after school, Zee and Ally went to the discount store to buy enough T-shirts for the band. By the time Chloe and Missy showed up at Zee's house, T-shirts in every color of the rainbow were spread across her bedroom floor.

Chloe sat cross-legged on the carpet, looking through a container of tiny plastic gems. "You and Jasper are so awesome together," she told Zee.

Zee gulped. "What do you mean?" she asked nervously. Had Chloe noticed that Zee was starting to have a crush on their best boy friend?

Chloe gave a little shrug. "You know, first you worked on Bluetopia together, then you came up with this cool costume idea together."

"Oh yeah," Zee agreed.

"I guess it makes sense since you're such good friends," Chloe went on.

"Mmm-hmm," Zee agreed, afraid to say more.

"We should make Marcus wear a pink shirt with tons of glitter," Missy said. Zee was happy that Missy changed the subject.

Chloe laughed. "I wonder if the Jonas Brothers have to make their own costumes."

"When we're as big as they are," Zee told her, "we won't even have to make our own beds."

Ally gestured to the twisted-up comforter on Zee's bed. "And your life would change how?" she asked.

"You know what I mean," Zee said, then looked around. "I still don't know if this is going to be my room once the twins are born." She looked over at Missy, hoping she might have something positive to say, but Missy was staring at the T-shirts on the floor.

"Hey, Missy!" Zee got her attention. "Did you have to give up anything big for your brothers?"

"Besides my hair?" Missy groaned.

Zee's stomach tightened. She wished that Missy would say, "Having twins around is awesome!"

Tap. Tap. Tap. Mrs. Carmichael interrupted the girls' conversation by knocking on the bedroom door.

"Come in, Mom," Zee said. She could see that her mother held a colorful roll of paper in each hand.

"I was hoping to get your opinion on something," Mrs. Carmichael began. "Which do you think would be better wallpaper for the babies' room—colorful stripes or the night sky?"

Ally and Missy said, "Colorful stripes" at the same time Zee and Chloe said, "The night sky."

Mrs. Carmichael shrugged and chuckled. "I guess I can't go wrong." She hummed as she held the samples against a wall, then turned to Zee. "Now I know you said you had to think about moving to the guest room, but I wanted to check these samples in this light—just in case."

Zee watched as her mother checked out the wallpaper from different angles. She wore a huge smile on her face. And when Mrs. Carmichael placed her hand on her stomach, Zee noticed that her mom was starting to get a little round belly. Zee began to feel guilty about the way she had been feeling. Why couldn't she be excited for her parents?

Still, these babies were going to change Zee's life completely. Was it so horrible of her to want to keep her bedroom the same?

That night, Zee logged onto Bluetopia. Landon had sent her a cupid teddy. Zee sighed. She decided that she needed to tell him she really didn't like him like that. But how?

Zee clicked to open her blog. "If you've got a problem . . . solve it," she sang as she waited for the page to load. "You don't have a reason . . . to quit." She stopped singing as the page opened. "That's it!" she shouted.

Zee just needed to solve her problems. Then they'd stop

being problems. Landon and the babies weren't going away, but that didn't mean she couldn't do something about them.

Hi, Bloggest One,

How can something that makes my mother so happy make me so sad? The babies are all she thinks about. Maybe I'm miserable *because* she's so happy.

I've decided the babies can be the stars in the Carmichael house. I want to be a rock star in the music world. If The Beans do really well tomorrow, maybe we'll start getting even more offers. Gigs. A recording contract! A NATIONAL TOUR!! Maybe Ally is right, and we can tour France with her. If that happens, I won't have to worry about the babies at all. I won't even be here.

And I'll get to be with Jasper even more. That's another problem I've figured out. I'll let him decide if we're just friends or if we should be more. Since there's no way I'll actually ask him, I'll have to watch what he says and does. I'm too scared to tell him I like him!

Which leads me to the other problem . . . I need to tell Landon I *don't* like him anymore. I mean, I do like him. I just don't like like him. A ton of girls have crushes on him. I don't want him to waste his time on me.

Then again . . . what if Jasper doesn't like me like that? Will I completely blow my chances with Landon? Do I care?

Oh no! I thought I was in problem-solving mode, but now I think I made even more!! ☹

Zee

As Zee clicked out of her blog, she noticed that just about everyone she knew was hanging out on Bluetopia. She had never seen the site so busy. Buds kept IMing her, swapping clothes, inviting her to play games, and sending her gifts.

Zee smiled. Bluetopia was a huge success! If The Beans became half as popular as Bluetopia, they'd be a worldwide phenomenon.

14
Brookdale Day Disaster

Chloe yawned.

"Are you tired?" Zee asked.

"I guess José and I were up too late chatting," she said. "But he's so interesting that the time went by really fast."

"Do you *like* him?" Zee asked.

A smile spread across Chloe's face. "Kind of."

"That's so cool," Zee cheered. "Too bad he lives so far away."

"Luckily, thanks to Bluetopia I can chat with him."

"I wish we could meet him," Zee said. "It just seems strange."

"I think it's romantic," Ally said. The girls were riding bikes over to Jasper's house so they could go to Brookdale Day together. "I mean, he found you on Bluetopia. If Jasper had never created it, you wouldn't even know he existed. It's fate."

"I hadn't even thought of it that way," Chloe said with a sigh. "I do kind of feel like we were meant to be together."

"I guess it's hard to be together when there's a whole ocean between you," Zee said.

"Don't worry, Chloe," Ally assured her. "If it's meant to be, that ocean won't stand between you for long."

"I hope you're right," Chloe said as the girls pedaled into Jasper's driveway.

Mrs. Chapman opened the door. "Hi, ladies," she said, then motioned toward the back of the house. "Jasper's in the office."

The three girls headed down the hall. Now that Zee had figured out she'd let Jasper decide if they should be more than friends, the thought of being near him didn't make her panic—although she still planned to watch for clues.

In the office, Jasper's fingers pecked furiously on the computer keyboard. He didn't even notice when the girls came in. *Clue one: Doesn't notice me when I come into the room. Conclusion: Just friends.*

"Jasper," Zee said.

"Aaaiiiieee!" Jasper jumped and his hands flew every which way.

"Sorry," Zee said as Chloe and Ally doubled over with laughter. "What are you doing?"

"I'm just making a couple of small adjustments to Blue-topia," Jasper told them.

"Well, hurry and finish!" Chloe commanded. "We don't want to be late for Brookdale Day."

"Don't rush me," Jasper said. "I need to fix a couple of glitches. Anyway, there's lots of time before we perform."

"But there's a ton of stuff to do there," Chloe pointed out. "I want to hit the craft tables. I might get some ideas for stuff to make."

"Me too," Zee said. "The rest of The Beans said they

were getting there early, too."

"We can meet up with them," Ally said.

"And give them their T-shirts," Zee added. She reached into her backpack, pulled out a green T-shirt with "Chapman" stenciled on the back, and tossed it onto the desk next to Jasper.

Jasper looked at it and smiled. "Thanks," he said to Zee warmly. *Clue two: Smiles and thanks me when I give him something. Conclusion: Inconclusive. He's very polite.*

"Come on! I want to find out what the big surprise is that Mr. P told us about," Ally told Jasper.

"Me too!" Zee and Chloe said at once.

"All right," Jasper said. "I suppose the rest of the fixes can wait until later." He hit a few keys, turned off the computer, and quickly pulled on the T-shirt.

"Yay!" Zee said. "Let's go!"

Jasper said good-bye to his parents and grabbed his bike. The group headed to downtown Brookdale where the festivities were taking place. The main street was closed off to everyone except pedestrians, so they locked their bikes to the rack and moved through the crowd.

Tables with jewelry, pottery, and paintings lined the street. The smell of spices, sauces, and sweets filled the air. Children were getting their faces painted to look like tigers and dogs.

"Look!" Chloe said, pointing to a banner stretched over the downtown park: WELCOME TO BLUETOPIA!

"Crikey!" Jasper exclaimed.

"Cool beans!" Zee rushed in that direction. "That must be the surprise Mr. P told us about!" Under the banner, people were crowded around computers that sat on long tables. Web pages were projected onto large screens above the computers. Kathi had her hand over her mouth while Jen talked frantically. Missy was sitting at one of the computers. It looked as though she was hitting the delete key over and over. Behind her, Marcus and Conrad laughed while Landon looked on with his arms crossed.

"Jasper, you're famous!" Chloe said as they followed behind Zee. "Bluetopia is your creation!"

But as they got closer, Zee could tell something was wrong. People were pointing at the screens. Some were gasping while others laughed.

The group hurried closer. "What's going on?" Ally asked.

"I can't tell," Zee said. "But I'm getting a funny feeling about this."

"I'm not sure I want to be famous," Jasper said.

That's when Zee saw one of her blog entries flash across one of the giant screens:

> My parents are trying to get me out of the way already.

Ohmylanta! Zee panicked. *No one else was supposed to see that.*

At the other end of the display, there was a loud screech. Zee recognized it right away—Kathi. Zee looked up to see a doodle from the Dish Club:

> Roxy is THE WORST cousin and THE WORST teacher I have ever had. I despise her!! And it's so gross the way that Zee is always trying to be teacher's pet. Blech!

Did everyone think that Zee was trying to be the teacher's pet? She had just wanted to learn more about music. She had to admit she liked all the attention now that her mother was so preoccupied, but she was just being herself.

A note from Missy to Conrad scrolled onto the screen.

> I want to be friends with Zee, but she only wants to talk to me about what it's like to have twin brothers. It gets kind of boring.

When Zee looked up, Missy was staring right at her. She quickly spun and looked the other way.

Chloe pushed through the crowd to one of the computers. She clicked around, then turned to Zee. "The Spanish boy is

really Marcus!" she exclaimed. Until that moment, Zee had never seen tough Chloe cry. The tears poured out of her eyes. "I really liked him, and he thought I was a joke!" she bawled.

Zee hugged Chloe. Looking over Chloe's shoulder, she could see Marcus and Conrad. They stood with their mouths wide-open and a guilty look on their faces.

Ally came over to Chloe and Zee. "Chloe, I wouldn't be too worried about it," she said, then locked eyes with Zee. "At least no one is talking about how much she hates your friends!"

"I don't hate them, Ally," Zee corrected her. "I just don't think they should have said those things about me."

Looking at the screens, Zee could see that now people in France and England were noticing that everything anyone had written on Bluetopia was appearing for everyone to see.

Then the accusations and apologies from the people who were logged on started to appear.

> How could you say that about me?

one French girl asked.

> I'm sorry I hurt your feelings,

someone in England doodled.

Ohmylanta! Zee thought. Panic twisted and turned in her stomach, then warmed her face. She remembered all the private thoughts that Brookdale—and the world—were reading. *Putting my blog online may have been my* worst *idea* ever.

Kathi raced over to Zee with a huge smile on her face and Jen followed close behind. "I can't believe you have a crush on Jasper!" she cheered.

Landon was standing nearby. "You have a crush on *him?*" he asked.

Chloe lifted her head. "On Jasper?" she asked enthusiastically through her sniffles.

Jasper looked at Zee. "On *me?*" he said in a near whisper. Then he cast his glance down and kicked at the grass with his feet.

"Ohmylanta!" Zee said, looking from one person to the next. How could she do this to herself? She might as well have copied pages of her diary and given them out to the entire school—or the world.

Ally planted her fists on her waist. "Well, it's a good thing you like British people, because you obviously hate French people."

"That's not fair," Zee responded. "They were mean to me first." She turned to Missy. "I didn't know that talking about the twins bothered you. I just liked having something in common. I wish you would have told me."

Landon interrupted. "You don't have a right to be mad at Missy," Landon said. "You lied to me."

"I did not," Zee protested.

"You made me think you liked me. Everyone knows you have a crush on me!"

Jasper suddenly looked up. "You have a crush on him?"

"How could you not know that?" Jen asked. "You're, like, one of her best friends."

"I guess we know why she didn't want to tell Jasper!" Kathi taunted.

"Just be quiet, Kathi!" Chloe yelled at her.

"Why don't you?" Kathi barked back.

Soon everyone was yelling. Accusations and apologies were flying—even after the big screens overhead went black.

Mr. P and Ms. Vardolis had been setting up the stage. They rushed over to the chaos.

"What's going on?" Ms. Vardolis shouted above the noise.

The arguing continued—until Mr. P put his fingers to his lips and let out an earsplitting whistle.

The Beans stopped mid-fight.

"We thought that showcasing Bluetopia would be great

for everybody," Mr. P said calmly. "What happened?"

Jasper stepped forward. "It's all my fault," he said. "I was trying to improve the site this morning. I must have typed something in that made members' private information available to everyone."

"Thanks a lot, Jasper!" Jen said angrily.

"Yeah," Landon agreed. "I guess you're not so hot after all."

"There is no way I'm performing today," Kathi told Mr. P.

"Me neither," Jen announced. "I'm so out of here!"

"Me too!" echoed Zee and the rest of the group.

The Beans started to leave—in separate directions.

15
The Show Must Go On

Another loud whistle split the air. "Stop!" Mr. P shouted in a firm voice Zee had never heard before. "No one is going anywhere," he boomed.

Everyone froze. Zee wondered how long they would have to stand around feeling awkward. Ms. Vardolis finally spoke up. "I know you're upset," she said. "But right now that doesn't matter."

It matters to me! Zee thought. She had expected the assistant teacher to be more understanding.

"You worked really hard this week," Ms. Vardolis reminded them. "Are you going to throw that away?" Landon and Missy shook their heads. "Or would you rather show everyone what you can do?" Conrad and Marcus nodded yes. "Besides, you made a commitment to play at Brookdale Day. You may be upset, but you promised your town a show, and that's what it deserves." Chloe and Ally shifted awkwardly from foot to foot. "You're a real band, and real musicians don't let their audiences down."

Zee looked from one band member to the next. *We are a real band.* "We should sing," she said. "We'll never be a professional band if we don't act like professionals."

"That's the spirit, Mackenzie," Ms. Vardolis said. "Just like a leader."

Ohmylanta! Zee thought. Kathi was looking at Ms. Vardolis, squinting her eyes and squeezing her lips together. The last thing The Beans needed right now was to remind Kathi how impressed Ms. Vardolis was with Zee.

Chloe and Jasper moved closer to Zee, and Ally gave a little nod. But the other band members shifted in their places and looked at the ground.

"Roxy's right!" Kathi suddenly blurted out.

"She is?" Jen asked.

"It would be stupid to let Bluetopia ruin everything," Kathi said. "More than it already has, that is. Right, Jen?"

Jen nodded. "Definitely!" She turned to Marcus.

Marcus looked over at Chloe. "I'm in," he announced. "What about you?" he asked Conrad.

One by one, The Beans headed across the park to the stage.

Once they had gotten there, Kathi turned to Zee. "*That's* leadership."

Zee had to agree with Kathi. She had gotten the group back together—even if it was just because she wanted to make Zee look bad.

The instruments, microphones, and amplifiers were already set up. "The only thing missing is the band," Zee said.

"And the cool T-shirts," Ally said, pointing to Zee's backpack.

"I almost forgot." Zee slid the backpack to the ground and started handing out the T-shirts to the rest of the group.

"Cool," Marcus said quietly as Zee handed him his.

Landon took his. "Thanks."

"This was such a great idea, Zee," Missy told her, pulling her orange tee over her head.

Things weren't back to normal, but they were better than they had been fifteen minutes before.

Mr. P stepped onto the stage. "Hello, Brookdale!" he announced. A cheer went up from the small crowd that had gathered on the grass. As he began thanking the Brookdale Day committee, people slowly moved over from the vendors and food stands to find their place on blankets and lawn chairs.

Then Mr. P was ready to announce the main event. "We are pleased to kick off Brookdale Day with a hometown band."

"Woo-hoo!" someone in the audience hooted.

"All right!" another person yelled.

The crowd made Zee feel better. She noticed that the rest of The Beans were starting to smile.

"I'm pleased to introduce to you—" Mr. P continued. "The Beans!"

The audience applauded politely. With Zee leading the group, The Beans hurried onto the stage. The others followed behind and picked up their instruments. Zee looked out at the faces in front of her. As she scanned the crowd, she saw her mother waving. Zee smiled. Her smile grew bigger when Adam gave her a thumbs-up.

Zee pivoted around to look at the others. "Are you ready?" she mouthed. They nodded. "One, two, three, four!" she counted off loudly.

On the beat, The Beans started playing. At first, they had some trouble with timing, and Zee was afraid they might fall apart altogether. But little by little, as people filled in the empty spots on the grass and started clapping along, they played better. By the end of the first song, there was even a small group of girls dancing with one another.

Zee tried to remember everything that had worked in rehearsals and everything that hadn't. But it wasn't until Zee thought about the fun everyone had had with the karaoke machine that the music fell into place.

By the final song, The Beans were as amazing as they had been during rehearsal. Zee got so caught up in the music, she completely forgot about Bluetopia, her crush on Jasper, and Landon's crush on her. When they finished their set, people rushed the stage.

"You were amazing!" one girl told Kathi.

"Thanks!" Kathi beamed.

"I want to download your CD," another girl told Missy.

Zee stopped signing autographs long enough to look over at Jasper. She felt a little tug as girls waited for a chance to talk to him. She was embarrassed when he looked over and saw her staring, but the feeling went away when he smiled.

Marcus interrupted Zee's thoughts. "Pretty good for a band that was broken up half an hour ago," he said, nudging Chloe.

Chloe put her arm around Ally. "Pretty good for any band!"

"Yeah, I'm glad we're all friends again," Landon said, staring right at Zee.

"The Beans are the best friends I have," Zee said.

"You're right about that," Missy put in.

Zee searched the crowd for her parents and was shocked to see Kathi's parents pushing their way through. "How could you do this to us?" Mrs. Barney asked her daughter.

"Um . . . I . . . don't know," Kathi responded. From the scared expression on her face, Zee could tell that Kathi had no idea what her parents were talking about.

"You publicly humiliated us when you said those things about Roxy," Mr. Barney said.

"You made the family look bad," Mrs. Barney added.

Kathi shrunk back from her parents. "But those notes were supposed to be private. I didn't expect anyone to see them."

"Well, they did, and I'm sure they'll have a fabulous time talking about this little incident at the tennis club."

Ms. Vardolis suddenly burst into the group. She leaned in and kissed Kathi's mother on the cheek, then did the same to her father. "Aunt Roni and Uncle Skip! I didn't see you standing there. I am just so proud of Kathi. If it hadn't been for her today, we might not have had a show."

All three of the Barneys stared with their mouths wide-open.

"Really?" Kathi said.

"Do you mind if I borrow my cousin for a sec?" Ms. Vardolis asked the Barneys.

"Uh . . . no," Mrs. Barney stammered. "Go ahead."

With a relieved look on her face, Kathi followed her cousin. "Thanks," Zee heard her say as they walked past.

"I owe you," Ms. Vardolis told her. Even though she wasn't trying, Zee could hear most of their conversation. "I was very impressed with how you got The Beans onstage today—especially since I know you've been pretty mad at me."

"How'd you guess?" Kathi joked, glancing over at the blank screens.

Ms. Vardolis laughed and put her arm around Kathi's shoulder. "I expected a lot from you because I know how incredibly talented you are. But I'm sorry I didn't praise you more for what you do well."

"You think I'm talented?" Kathi asked.

"I've always admired you. Ever since you were born, my mother has told me you were the cutest baby and you sang the sweetest." Ms. Vardolis leaned a little closer to Kathi. "When I was a teenager, I even tried to straighten my hair so it would be more like yours."

"My mom wanted mine to be curly like yours!" Kathi gasped.

"Today I realized I was unfair to ask so much of you," Ms. Vardolis went on. "After all, that's what everyone did to me when I was your age. I'm sorry."

Then Zee heard Kathi say something she'd never heard her say before. "I'm sorry, too." She hugged Ms. Vardolis.

By now, the crowd was settling down and the next band was getting ready to go onstage.

"Heads up, Beans!" Mr. P shouted, motioning for everyone to gather around him. "You all did a fabulous job today. And I think you learned a valuable lesson about teamwork. So don't give up on The Beans and don't give up on Bluetopia."

"You don't want us to get rid of Bluetopia?" Jasper asked.

"Just because something has a couple of problems doesn't mean you have to get rid of it," Mr. P told him. "If you only focus on what went wrong, you'll never accomplish anything."

"But a lot went wrong," Conrad pointed out.

"And a lot went right, too," Mr. P said. "We featured Bluetopia because of all the great things about it. You created a place for people all over the world to hang out and get to know one another. Now you guys should talk about what you liked about Bluetopia and start from there."

"All right!" Jasper agreed.

Marcus walked over to Chloe. "I didn't mean to make fun of you," he said. "I like you."

"You do?"

"You're really cool and funny," Marcus explained. "That's why I thought it was okay to joke around with you."

"Whose photo was that?" Chloe asked.

"Some model," Marcus said. "I got it off the internet."

"Too bad! He was really cute!" Chloe wiggled her eyebrows up and down.

Seeing Chloe forgive Marcus so easily gave Zee courage. She walked over to Missy. "I'm sorry all I ever wanted to talk about with you was the twins. But that's not the reason I wanted to be friends."

Missy ran her fingers through her hair. "Well, it's not like I didn't have a ton of complaints about them lately."

"Now at least we can also talk about what it's like to have short hair," Zee pointed out.

Missy laughed.

After Zee and Ally rode their bikes home, Ally said she had some things to do on the computer. "Not Bluetopia, I hope," Zee joked.

"No way!" Ally assured.

Zee went into the TV room and flopped on the couch in an exhausted heap.

"Hello, Zee." Mrs. Carmichael came into the room and sat next to Zee.

Zee sat up. "Hi, Mom."

"Adam told me that you weren't so thrilled about the twins after all," Zee's mom continued.

"I can't believe he told you!" Zee said. "That was supposed to be private." Inside Zee was more nervous than angry. Would her mother think she was a spoiled brat?

"I know you didn't mean for me to find out, but I'm glad I did," Mrs. Carmichael explained. "I had no idea I was acting so crazy."

"I guess I was acting a little crazy, too," Zee said. "I thought you might forget about me once the twins were here."

"I may forget a few things—like snacks and rehearsals—but I will never forget about you," Mrs. Carmichael promised. "You're my Zee."

Zee smiled and squeezed her mother in a hug. Then she remembered the babies and let go. "Am I squeezing too tight?"

"Never!" her mother said, holding on even tighter.

When they stopped hugging, Zee said, "I think I would like to move into the guest room."

"Are you sure?"

"Can I give it a total Zee makeover?"

Zee's mother smiled and nodded. Then she hugged Zee again.

Zee raced upstairs to tell Ally what had happened. When she stepped into her bedroom, Ally was sitting on her bed with the laptop.

"What are you doing?" Zee asked.

Ally stopped typing. "Emailing my friends in France."

"Oh," Zee said quietly.

"Do you want to read what I wrote?"

Zee wasn't sure what to say. She couldn't believe those girls had said such mean things about her and caused Ally and Zee to fight on their last day together. But Zee didn't want to fight anymore. "Sure," she said, and began to read the screen.

Hi, guys,

I had such a great time in the U.S. with my BFF Zee. I got to do all of the awesome stuff we always used to do together. Here's what I'll miss most about her.

She's incredibly nice. She's miserable if she thinks she's hurt someone's feelings.

She's really talented. She's an amazing guitar player and singer. She writes awesome songs, too.

She's funny. We spent a ton of the time laughing.

And she has great fashion sense. I know because sometimes we dress the same!

I can't wait for you to meet her.

C u soon!

Au revoir,

A

"Thanks!" Zee said when she'd finished reading.

"Anything for my BFF!" Ally logged out of her email.

"Can I use the computer now?" Zee asked.

"Sure. What are you going to do?"

"I wanted to chat with Jasper about Bluetopia," Zee explained.

"Oh yeah!" Ally said. "Why didn't you tell me you have a crush on Jasper?"

"'Cause I'm not sure I do." Zee paused. "But I'm not sure I don't."

"Why not?" Ally asked.

"I don't want to mess up our friendship," Zee said. "And I don't know if he likes me like that."

"I wish one of you would fess up and find out!" Ally said frantically.

Zee laughed and signed on to chat with Jasper.

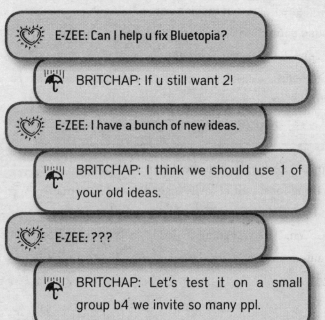

E-ZEE: Can I help u fix Bluetopia?

BRITCHAP: If u still want 2!

E-ZEE: I have a bunch of new ideas.

BRITCHAP: I think we should use 1 of your old ideas.

E-ZEE: ???

BRITCHAP: Let's test it on a small group b4 we invite so many ppl.

Zee and Jasper continued chatting about Bluetopia and The Beans' concert. Nobody mentioned the crush, so when they finally said good-bye, Zee had no idea where she stood.

Hi, Diary,

You won't believe what happened! Let's just say that when it comes to my secrets, you're the only diary I'm talking to from now on.

I thought I wasn't sure if I like Jasper or not, but now I am sure. I do like him. I mean like like him. But I can also be his friend. I don't have to go crazy when I see him or think about him.

Maybe he doesn't like me back. I can live with that. I've still got a great friend. There's no guy like Jasper! Landon's nice, but I just liked him because he was so cute. We're not interested in the same things. And now I know that's really important to me. Thanks to Jasper.

Zee

16

The Good-bye

At the Los Angeles airport, Zee wiped a tear from her cheek. "I'm going to miss you so much!" she told Ally, hugging her—again.

Ally blew her nose into a tissue. "I had such an awesome visit. I wish we could still hang out like that all the time."

"We will," Zee promised. "When I come visit you in France."

Ally got a concerned look on her face.

"What's wrong?" Zee asked.

"I'm just afraid you really won't want to come—after what my friends did," Ally explained. "I'm sorry I didn't stick up for you sooner."

"Why didn't you?" Zee asked.

"Because you've always been there for me no matter what," Ally said. "You've always forgiven me."

"Luckily, you always forgive me, too." Zee smiled.

"That's the problem with my new friends. They make a big deal out of everything. I guess I was kind of scared of them."

"Are you scared of them now?" Zee asked.

"No, they thought the email was really cool and can't wait to meet you!"

"Flight three-twenty-two to Charles de Gaulle Airport now boarding gate six," the announcement called the passengers on Ally's plane.

"Oh no!" Zee said. She gave Ally another hug. "Goodbye."

Zee waved as Ally slowly walked toward the gate.

"You and Jasper have to get Bluetopia going again so we can keep in touch constantly," Ally called across the waiting area.

Zee laughed and called back, "We will." She watched her friend disappear down the long corridor to the plane.

Zee was quiet on the ride back to Brookdale. She was thinking about the email she would send her best friend.

Ally,

I miss you soooooooooo much.

Next time I will see you in Paris. Promise to show me the most delicious pastries, coolest shops, and cutest guys. Ooh-la-la!

Until then, see you on Bluetopia!

LYLAS,

Zee

Then Zee got out her guitar and started writing her next song: "Double Trouble."

Online Glossary

&	and
@	at
<3 (sideways heart)	= love (<33 = extra love)
=	equal
1	one
1st	first
2	to; two; too
2day	today
2-faced	two-faced
2gether	together
2morrow	tomorrow
2nite	tonight
4	for
411	information
4get	forget
4give	forgive
4gotten	forgotten
ASAP	as soon as possible
b	be

b/c	because
b/f	boyfriend
b4	before
BB4N	bye-bye for now
BFF	best friends forever
bz	busy
c	see
CA	California
cld	could
every1	everyone
g/f	girlfriend
gr8	great
GTG	gotta go
GTR	gotta run
H&K	hugs and kisses
K	okay
LOL	laughing out loud
LYLAS	love you like a sister
M	am
mayb	maybe
mins	minutes
MUSM	miss you so much
NK	no kidding
no1	no one

NP	no problem
nt	not
OMG	oh, my God
OMGYG2BK	oh, my God, you've got to be kidding
pic	picture
pls	please
r	are
rm	room
thm	them
thx	thanks
TTFN	ta-ta for now
u	you
u'll	you'll
ur	your; you're
urs	yours
w	with
w/o	without
WB	write back
WFM	works for me
ws	was
y	why

Acknowledgments

I must first say a big thank-you to my entire Harper team: Erica Sussman, Sarah Barley, Tara Weikum, Susan Katz, Elise Howard, Kate Jackson, Diane Naughton, Cristina Gilbert, Laura Kaplan, and Marisa Russell. You've made this experience a pleasure as always.

Kate Lee, words can't express the gratitude I have for all the work you've done on my behalf. It's such a pleasure to work with you. Sam Wilson, thank you so much for your great work and advice—you're always a great advocate for me!

To my family: Mom, Dad, Adrianne, Erica, Marcus, Lisa, and William—thank you all for being there for me and supporting me through this process. I couldn't do it without you!

To all of my dear friends: Thank you for keeping me sane and sharing your passion for my books with your friends and family.

Finally, to all the teachers and librarians who love these books and invite me into your schools, I give you the greatest thanks.

Read on for a sneak peek at Mackenzie's next adventure!

Double Trouble

1

The Big Move

"Umm . . . Zee?" Chloe Lawrence-Johnson raised an eyebrow as she held up an old sock with one googly eye and a Magic Marker mouth. She had found it while cleaning off the top of a bookcase in the bedroom of her best friend, Mackenzie Blue Carmichael.

"Cool beans!" Zee cried. "I have been wondering where Mr. Sock was."

"For how long?" Chloe asked her friend. She looked down at Zee from the top of the step stool she was standing on. "Five years?"

"Probably." Zee rushed over to Chloe to take the puppet. She shook off the dust. "When I move into my new room, I'm going to make up for lost time and give him a place of honor where everyone can see him."

"Uh-huh," Chloe said skeptically. "Maybe until he gets buried in an avalanche of clothes."

"No way! I'm turning over a new leaf," Zee responded. "Now that I'm going to be a big sister to twins, I'm going to have to be way more responsible. Out with Zee the Messy, in with Zee the—"

"Well, it *is* true you're not going to be the baby of the family anymore," Chloe interrupted, smiling. She glanced around Zee's room. Zee's school uniform lay on the floor, and her comforter was heaped in a pile in the middle of Zee's unmade bed. "But it's hard to change overnight."

Zee adjusted the bright green bandana that she had wrapped around her short red hair. "It doesn't need to be overnight. The twins aren't due for a few months!"

"If you say so," Chloe said, stepping off the stool to pick up a headless Barbie jammed between the bookcase and the wall. "All of your books are packed. What do you want me to do now?"

Zee began to peel her Jonas Brothers poster from the wall. "Can you help me take this down?"

"Are you going to get rid of it?" Chloe reached up to loosen a corner. "It's autographed!"

"I've had this poster forever. It belongs in the Old Zee's room."

"What will New Zee put up?"

Zee squinted as she thought. "Maybe I'll get a Dakota Morning poster—since she's my favorite actor."

"Do you think you can get her to sign a poster, too?"

"*That* would be amazingly incredible!" Zee said. Once the Jonas Brothers poster was off the wall, Zee scanned the room. Her eyes fell on the closed closet door. "How about if we start packing up the closet together?"

As Zee flung open the doors, Chloe's eyes grew wide. Every shelf was piled high with clothes, games, and art supplies. "Zee! Don't you ever get rid of anything?"

"I've never had to," Zee answered with a shrug. "I've lived in this room my whole life."

Chloe smiled. "I know what you mean. When we moved from Atlanta last summer, my parents made me give away a ton of stuff from my childhood."

"No way! Do you miss it?" Zee asked.

Chloe tilted her head and said, "I thought I would. But now, not really."

Zee took a box down from a shelf. "Well, you're the best person to help me decide what to keep and what to throw away or donate," she said.

"Knock, knock!" Ginny Carmichael, Zee's mother, called out as she stepped into Zee's room.

"We're in the closet!" Zee called to her mother, and then shouted, "I don't believe it!"

"What?" Mrs. Carmichael hurried over to the closet to find Zee clutching a tattered old blanket and a furless stuffed bunny.

Chloe pointed at the bunny. "Lemme guess. That's Mr. Rabbit."

"No," Zee said, hugging the animal tighter. "Mr. Long Ears."

"And your baby blanket!" Mrs. Carmichael said.

Chloe reached into a half-full box and pulled out a pair of small white leather shoes. "And here are your baby shoes!" she cried.

"And my baby album," Zee said, lifting a stuffed album out of the box.

Sitting between Mrs. Carmichael and Chloe on her bed, Zee began turning the pages and commenting on the photos. Some were taken before she was even born. In the first picture, Zee's mother was still pregnant.

"I'd forgotten how enormous I was with you!" Mrs. Carmichael said with a laugh.

"Look at how long your hair was, Mom!"

"Oh my gosh, Mrs. Carmichael! Is this your baby

shower?" Chloe pointed to a picture of a pregnant Mrs. Carmichael sitting in a comfortable armchair and surrounded by women and a stack of presents. A giant pink cake with a white stork in the center sat on the low table in front of her.

"My best friends threw me showers for both Zee and Adam," Mrs. Carmichael explained. "That was before we moved to California. Do you remember visiting them in New York, Zee—Monica Flores and Joanne O'Neill?"

"Oh, yeah," Zee said, thinking back to the trip. It felt so long ago now. She was barely in the first grade.

"Are your friends going to throw you a shower again?" Chloe wondered aloud.

Mrs. Carmichael looked at both Zee and Chloe and shook her head slightly. "It's not traditional to throw a shower for the third"—Zee's mother looked down at her large belly—"or fourth baby."

"But with twins, there's twice as much to celebrate!" Chloe said, nudging Mrs. Carmichael. "No offense, Zee."

"That doesn't offend me at all," Zee said, then stood up. "Actually, that gives me an idea . . ."

"What?" Chloe and Mrs. Carmichael asked at the same time.

Zee bounced excitedly in place. "We'll throw you a baby shower!"

Mrs. Carmichael laughed and said, "Oh, Zee, you've got so much going on already."

"The only things I have to worry about right now are school and The Beans," Zee said. "That's practically nothing!"

"Hey!" Chloe's high ponytail swung around her head as she jumped up from the bed. "The Beans could perform at the shower!"

"Cool idea!" Zee exclaimed. "This is going to be the best baby shower ever! It won't be a regular shower at all—it'll be a Baby Blast!"

"Can I help you plan it, Zee?" Chloe asked.

"Definitely! Let's go get some snacks and start coming up with our ideas."

The girls were starting to leave Zee's room when Mrs. Carmichael called after them, "I thought you were going to clean your closet!"

"I will. I promise!" Zee called back. "We just need to talk about a few ideas first—for the most fantabsome baby shower in the history of the world!"

"How about if we figure out a theme, then plan everything else around that?" Zee said, grabbing a handful of popcorn from a nearby bowl. She was stretched out on the couch in her family's TV room.

"Awesome!" Chloe said from the floor, where she sat with her back against the sofa. "We just have to figure out what your mother likes."

"She likes to cook," Zee said.

"Yeah! It could be a cooking party!"

"Except I wouldn't want to make her cook at her shower."

"True. We should keep thinking."

Zee tried to focus on Baby Blast ideas, but her mind kept wandering. The day before, she and Chloe had performed with their band, The Beans, at Brookdale Day, a huge festival in town. The event was the first to feature Bluetopia, the social networking site that their best friend Jasper Chapman had created. Kids all around the world were signed up for the site! Unfortunately, Bluetopia had a glitch, and a lot of the users' secrets were revealed—including Zee's maybe-crush on Jasper. Zee and Chloe hadn't discussed the not-so-secret secret all morning, and Zee really needed her best friend to help her sort it all out.

"This is so much fun, right?" Zee blurted out. "You and me. Me and you. Just us girls. Planning a shower."

"Uh-huh . . ." Chloe said, turning around to look at Zee.

Zee tried again. "It's good for it to be just us—you know, without any guys—like Jasper."

"But we do things all the time without Jasper," Chloe

reminded Zee. "He never comes to Wink! with us when we get manicures.

"True. Guys and girls really are incredibly different."

Chloe shrugged. "I don't know. We also have a lot in common."

"I guess I'm just wondering if a girl can ever *really* be best friends with a guy. Do you ever wonder about that?" Zee asked, her voice rising.

Chloe stared at Zee without blinking. "Nope," she said matter-of-factly. "Jasper's one of my best friends—just like you. It's not like with Marcus—or Landon."

Chloe had had a crush on Marcus Montgomery since she met him at the beginning of the year. And Zee had had one on Landon Beck since she could remember. Lately, it had grown clear that Landon liked Zee, too. The only problem was, Zee wasn't really sure if she still felt that way about *him* anymore—which the Bluetopia blowup also revealed.

"But I'm sure Jasper would rather spend the day fixing Bluetopia than planning a shower," Chloe continued. "Although he's such a neat freak, he probably would have loved the chance to finally clean your room!"

"Hey!" Zee playfully knocked Chloe in the head with a sofa cushion. "It's not *that* bad," she said, then sheepishly added, "Is it?"

<u>Baby Blast Themes</u>

Western—Mom's afraid of horses (although I look cute in cowboy hats!)

Beach—Brookdale is right near the ocean, so that's not so exotic for us

Pajamas—This probably wouldn't be as much fun for Mom's friends as it would be for mine

Wacky hats—See "Pajamas"

Hi, Diary.

As you can see, that's ↑ the list of themes that Chloe and I came up with for the Baby Blast. And as you can also see, none of them is perfect. Mom deserves something special—really special. (After all, she's the greatest mother in the world!) Chloe and I are going to keep thinking, but we better figure it out soon. Before you know it, the babies will be here. Which means . . .

Good news: I'm going to be a big sister very soon!

Bad news: I need to plan a shower—fast!

Good news: I've got Chloe.

Bad news: Chloe didn't say one thing about everyone finding out that I MIGHT have a crush on Jasper.

(OK, that has NOTHING to do with twins or planning a shower, but I didn't know how else to bring it up.)

Chloe, Jasper, and I are like peanut butter and jelly—and bread. We go together. So it would be really weird if I had a crush on him. Or would it? I mean, maybe Chloe didn't talk about it because she doesn't think it's such a big deal.

I used to think Landon was the cutest boy ever. I could barely think straight when he was around. But now I don't think I like him that way anymore. He's cute, but we don't seem to have anything to talk about. It's all pretty confusing and weird. Isn't it?

Zee